CLAUDIA KISHI,
LIVE ON AIR

I had written in my essay that I had good ideas flying around my brain. I had exaggerated. A lot.

Now what? Should I bring tapes to the interview? A list of talk-show-type topics? A list of people to interview? Or was this supposed to be a phone-in show?

What had I got myself into?

That night I had nightmares. The whole world was listening to WSTO. Kids riding bikes and wearing headphones. Shoppers in malls. A capacity crowd in a sports arena with enormous speakers on stage, wailing: "And now, WSTO presents what you've all been waiting for—Claudia Kishi!"

And then, dead silence.

By morning I must have sweated off ten pounds.

CLAUDIA KISHI, LIVE ON AIR

Ann M. Martin

Hippo

*The author gratefully acknowledges
Peter Lerangis
for his help in
preparing this manuscript.*

Scholastic Children's Books,
Commonwealth House, 1–19 New Oxford Street,
London, WC1A 1NU, UK
a division of Scholastic Ltd
London ~ New York ~ Toronto ~ Sydney ~ Auckland

First published in the US by Scholastic Inc., 1995
First published in the UK by Scholastic Ltd, 1997

ISBN 0 590 19370 8

Typeset by Rowland Phototypesetting Ltd,
Bury St Edmunds, Suffolk
Printed by Cox & Wyman Ltd, Reading, Berks.

10 9 8 7 6 5 4 3 2 1

1st CHAPTER

"So the bases are loaded, okay? The score is a tie, two outs—and the batter hits a slow grounder to Jake Kuhn at first. . ."

Kristy Thomas was talking.

And talking.

Me? I was working hard. Trying to keep my eyes open. If I fell asleep, my face would land in my lunch. And I did not want to go to my next class with hair full of corned beef in cream sauce.

Baseball is not my favourite topic. It's not rock bottom, but it's pretty close. If Kristy had been talking about spelling, or techniques of room cleaning, my nose would already have been in the beef.

"So what do you think Jake does?" Kristy looked around. Her face was all a-twinkle, as if we were on the edges of our seats.

1

Now, if you were talking, and you saw three droopy-eyed girls staring back at you, slowly chewing their meals, would you assume they were dying of suspense?

"Give up? *He fields the ball and runs home!*"

Chew, chew, chew. We raised our eyebrows and tried to seem fascinated.

"Maybe he had to go to the toilet," I suggested. "Those games are long."

Kristy looked at me blankly for a moment, then snapped, "Home *plate*, Claudia! You see, he wanted to stop the run, even though all he had to do was step on first. Which would have ended the game without a run scored!"

Oh.

The corned beef was looming closer.

Kristy, as you can guess, is a sports fanatic. She's the founder, manager, and head coach of Kristy's Krushers, a softball team for little kids.

Are you sitting down? I, Claudia Kishi, Dunce of All Sports, was once the co-coach of the Krushers. Yes, it's true. When Kristy joined the Stoneybrook Middle School softball team and didn't have time to coach, my friend Stacey McGill and I took her place.

It didn't help. I still don't know how to play the game.

"Well," Kristy said grumpily, "I suppose you just had to be there."

She took her fork and began shovelling in her lunch, as if she hadn't eaten for days.

"Ugh! Kristy, please eat with your mouth closed," Dawn said. "Who wants to watch you chew up murdered mammals?"

Kristy burst out laughing so hard, I thought she was going to throw up. *"Murdered mammals?"*

"Well, that meat in your mouth was once a living, feeling cow." Dawn lifted a forkful of lettuce and pointed it at Kristy for emphasis. "Have you ever seen photos of what happens inside a slaughterhouse? The poor, shivering beasts heading towards their death—"

"Dawn, please!" Mary Anne said.

I pushed my lunch aside. Suddenly I wasn't hungry.

Kristy shrugged. "Some people collect dolls. Some collect baseball cards. Dawn Schafer collects pictures of cow torture."

"Can we change the subject?" I asked.

"Yes!" Mary Anne agreed. "Er . . . Logan and I are making a tape tonight. You know, a collection of our favourite songs."

"I did that once," Kristy said.

"Thirty-two renditions of 'Take Me Out to the Ball Game'," I remarked. (Sorry, it just slipped out of my mouth.)

Kristy threw a bread roll at me.

Don't worry. Kristy and I are friends. If she didn't like me, she would have thrown something harder.

Actually, Kristy has thrown a lot of things at me over the years. We grew up living opposite each other here in Stoneybrook, Connecticut. My mum says Kristy used to bop me with her Raggedy Ann doll because I didn't learn to walk as fast as she did. (Figures!)

As I walked home from school that afternoon in the spring sunshine, my jacket slung over my shoulder, I wished Kristy still lived in her old house. On gorgeous afternoons like these, she had all kinds of great outdoorsy plans.

"Hi, Janine!" I called to my sister as I breezed in the front door and through the living room.

"Hello—" I was halfway up the stairs when Janine saw me. "Claudia, what on Earth are you wearing?"

Gulp!

I was wearing a back-to-front T-shirt, dungarees I'd made by sewing together two halves cut from different pairs, and odd socks. It was my "deconstructionist" look. You know, like the art movement. Those paintings that show you the parts of objects rearranged in interesting ways. Well, that was the idea, anyway. Cool, isn't it?

I am obsessed with art. Painting, sculpture, drawing, jewellery-making—I like creating in any medium. Including clothes. (This makes me definitely the odd one out in my family. My parents think shoes with tassels are daring.)

Janine shook her head, chuckling. "*Was that* why you wore your jacket to breakfast this morning? To cover that up so we wouldn't have indigestion?"

"I was *cold*." (Well, it was sort of true.)

Janine just shook her head and walked to her room.

Later I could hear the usual furious clacking of the computer keyboard coming from Janine's room. I tried to slip quietly past her open door, to avoid another comment.

"Hmm. Frankenstein's jumpsuit," I heard as I went into my bedroom.

Janine is disgustingly clever. Even if she lent me a quarter of her IQ points, I'd be brilliant and she'd still have enough left over to be a genius. She's at high school but takes college courses. And her taste in fashion runs to white blouses and grey pleated skirts.

Needless to say, my parents think she's perfect.

I've tried to be a high achiever like her. But 1) I can't spell, 2) computers hate me (and vice-versa), and 3) my eyes cross when I read anything more complicated than a Nancy Drew mystery.

Where did my artistic side come from? Probably my mum's mum, Mimi. She understood me better than anyone else. Mimi's English wasn't great (she immigrated to this country from Japan), but it didn't matter. We were on the same wavelength. She lived with us all my life and I loved her *so* much. When she died I was devastated.

Actually, one other person inherited the crazy, creative genes in my family—my aunt Peaches, Mimi's other daughter. (Her real name is Miyoshi. Her husband, my uncle Russ, gave her the nickname. Why? No one knows.) When Peaches was pregnant, she and Russ bought a house in Stoneybrook. While they waited for the occupants to move out, they lived with us for a month. It was a wild and mostly fun time, but it ended sadly. You see, Peaches had a miscarriage.

Russ and Peaches moved into their new

house anyway, and they're still planning to have another baby. Now Peaches works full-time. I really miss her.

Now our house is pretty quiet. Dull, if you want to know the truth. Except during Babysitters Club meetings, which are held in my room.

But you know what? With Stacey McGill gone, even those are less fun.

No, Stacey didn't move away. She resigned (or was fired, depending on who's telling the story, but more about that later).

Mimi, Peaches, Stacey. My three soulmates. Without them in my life, I was feeling rather low.

Not that I don't love my other BSC friends. I do. I'm lucky to have them. But you know how it is. You need that one extra-special person in your life.

Sigh!

Time for a pick-me-up. A definite Twix moment. I opened my desk drawer and peeped under a stack of looseleaf papers.

Only one packet of Milk Bottles and two Snickers bars.

I rummaged under my bed, where I discovered three bags of pretzels and some Chewits. I opened a few shoe boxes in my wardrobe, which contained M&M's and chocolate covered raisins and Yorkie bars and Doritos.

I eventually found a Twix among my art supplies. I ripped open the wrapper and ate it.

I felt much better.

Why do I hide my junk food? Because of my parents, also known as the Nutrition Police. They disapprove of unhealthy food, which is probably why I love it so much. Besides, I'm in pretty good shape, and I eat my dinner every night without complaining, so what's the diff?

As I chewed, I changed clothes. That afternoon I had a short sitting job at the Pikes'. They have eight kids (one of whom is a BSC member, thank goodness), so there's already enough deconstruction in that house.

Besides, I didn't want to hear any snide remarks on the way out.

Dressed in jeans and a button-down men's shirt over a stretch top, I walked to the Pikes'. I brought a Kid-Kit with me. (Well, sort of.) Kid-Kits are supposed to be boxes full of toys, games and activities for kids. (Kristy thought of the idea, and kids really do love them.) Mine, though, is filled with art supplies. It's more of an Art-Kit.

Slate Street was silent. This is unusual, because the Pikes live there. The neighbours must have been in shock.

Claire Pike, who's five, answered the door.

"Hi! Hi! Hi! Hi! Hi! Hi! Hi!" she squealed, jumping up and down.

"Come on in, Claudia!" Mallory Pike shouted from the playroom. Mal's the oldest Pike (eleven). She's the BSC member I mentioned. "We're having story time."

Claire raced into the playroom ahead of me. She sat on the floor next to her triplet brothers, Adam, Jordan and Byron Pike.

Yes, ten-year-old boy triplets. Yikes! Can you imagine? And that, of course, is just the beginning of the Pikes. The others are Vanessa (nine), Nicky (eight), Margo (seven) and Claire the Jumping Bean.

And they were all, *all*, staring quietly at Mallory and a hairy monster.

The hairy monster looked suspiciously like Ben Hobart, with a mask. (Ben is Mallory's boyfriend, more or less.)

"And so the horrible Oogly Oogly Beast searched high and low for his missing toothbrush," Mal read from a spiral notebook. "He had not brushed his teeth for days. . ."

"Ugh!" Bryon Pike said. "Bad breath!"

Behind Mal, Ben the Beast put his hands on his hips and tried to look angry.

Mal went on, and I listened. With her reddish-brown hair pulled back into a thick ponytail, and her big, round glasses, she looked older than eleven. Her story was about a monster who was obsessed with being clean. (Mal is a great writer and she wants to be a children's author/illustrator one day.)

I sat on the floor and started doodling. I tried to make some illustrations for Mallory's story, but they looked rather stupid. So I watched.

". . . So the Oogly Oogly Beast slowly approached the campers. Drool dripped from his mouth and on to his white fur. Then, bursting into the campsite, he shouted—"

Mallory paused. Ben froze in an attack position.

"What? What?" Vanessa demanded.

Mallory's eyes widened threateningly. Then she said, "'Er, excuse me, has anybody got some Wash'n'Go?'"

The kids cracked up.

Mallory grinned at Ben. I could hear him laughing behind his mask.

The two of them were very sweet. And

all of a sudden I had another reminder of why I was feeling rotten.

Boylessness.

Mary Anne had Logan. Mallory had Ben. Kristy (sort of) had this boy called Bart. Stacey, my ex-best friend, had a boyfriend called Robert.

Claudia? Zilch.

Not that I'm boy-crazy. It's no great tragedy not to have a boyfriend.

But it's no great honour either.

I've tried: I even put an ad in the Personals column in the Stoneybrook Middle School newspaper. I was *running* the column at the time, but that didn't help. The only people who answered my appeal for the "Perfect Boy" were Alan Gray (the class idiot) and Stacey McGill. (Yes, Stacey. She was feeling sorry for me.)

Sometimes I wish I were still working on the newspaper. At least I'd be meeting people.

"*Waaaaahhhhh!*" Ben was crying now.

"Poor, poor Oogly," Mallory said. "All those teeth and nothing to brush with. . ."

Poor, poor Claudia, I thought.

"No bath, no towel. . ."

No boyfriend, no best friend, no activities. . .

"So sad and lonely. . ."

So sad and lonely.

Please! Get a grip, Kishi.

I stood up and left the room. I tried to look nonchalant about it.

But I was feeling so sorry for myself!

By the time I got to the kitchen, I had made up my mind. I needed a change. I was going to do something new with my life. Something interesting. Fun. Different.

By the end of the day, I, Claudia Kishi, was going to turn my life around!

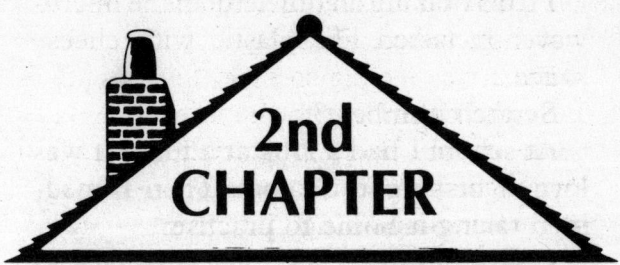

2nd CHAPTER

I lied.

My life was exactly the same, right through to the next day, Wednesday.

But I'd been trying. After I left the Pikes, I mentioned my problem at home. Janine suggested taking up computer programming. Dad brought up stamp collecting. Mum's response was, "Haven't you got any homework?"

Big help.

So I sat down and made a list of possible choices—the first things that came to mind, no matter how strange.

1. Juba
2. tap dancing
3. Cooking
4. coir choir
5. Swiming
6. dramma club

The next morning, I began testing the waters.

I tried making an omelette in the microwave. It tasted like plastic with cheese sauce.

Scratch number 3.

At school I had a look at a tuba. It was love at first sight. *So* cool. Then I imagined taking it home to practise.

Ugh! Number 1 was out. (I'd have to take weightlifting classes first.)

I asked the music teacher about choir, and she told me I needed to come in after school and sing for her. Alone.

I said thanks but no thanks. Cross out number 4.

I was going to talk to the captain of the SMS swimming team, till I looked at her chlorine-damaged hair. NFM! (*Not For Me*.)

Number 5 bit the dust.

That left tap and drama. I was once involved in a production of *Peter Pan*, but only as a set designer. And I knew nothing about tap. Luckily one of my BSC friends, Jessica Ramsey, is an excellent dancer. Several BSC members have sung and acted in shows. (Kristy played the lead in *Peter Pan*, and Shannon Kilbourne has starred in summer camp musicals.)

I decided to bring up choices 2 and 6 at the Babysitters Club meeting.

So after school, I went home and waited.

That's the nice thing about living in the exclusive headquarters of your club. Everyone comes to you. (And you are hardly ever late.)

What makes the Claudia Kishi bedroom so special? My scintillating personality? My superior art? My confectionery collection?

Well, yes, of course. But mostly my phone. I'm the only BSC member with a private line, which is crucial to our business.

Yes, business. We all have titles and duties. (I'm the vice-chairman and official out-of-hours phone answerer.) Our clients are Stoneybrook parents, who call us during our meeting times—five-thirty to six, every Monday, Wednesday and Friday. With one phone call, they reach six great babysitters. That's the way the BSC works.

I mean what a simple idea, isn't it? Wrong. No one had thought of it before Kristy Thomas.

Kristy is an Ideas Machine. I mean it. She is not normal. If she put her mind to it, she could work out how to de-stripe a tiger. She dreamed up the BSC one afternoon when her mum couldn't find a sitter for her little brother, David Michael.

Times were tough for Kristy's family back then. Mrs Thomas was bringing up four kids by herself—Charlie (who's now seventeen), Sam (fifteen) and David Michael (seven and a half). Kristy's dad had walked out on his family not long after David Michael was born, just left them flat, no explanations, no nothing. Can you imagine?

Things have really changed since then. Mrs Thomas married this nice, quiet guy called Watson Brewer, who is a millionaire. Now Kristy and her family live in a real mansion on the wealthy side of town, together with an adopted little sister, Emily Michelle, who's from Vietnam; Nannie, Kristy's grandmother; Watson's two kids from his previous marriage (seven-year-old Karen and four-year-old Andrew, who are there every other month); and several pets.

Now that Kristy lives so far away, she has to be driven to meetings by her brother, Charlie. Even so, she has hardly ever been late for a meeting. In fact, she's usually the first one there.

That day, she arrived at 5:24.

"Hey, Claudia, what's up?" she said,

sitting down in the director's chair near my desk. That's her usual spot. (Mine is on my bed, sitting cross-legged.)

"Kristy," I said. "I need an activity, something really interesting and fun. And don't tell me to take up a sport. What do you think I should do, tap dancing or drama?"

Kristy looked at me as if I'd suggested adding another nose to my face. "Are you serious? What about something like volleyball?"

Luckily Jessi Ramsey and Mallory Pike walked in the room then. Jessi's eleven, like Mal. They are our two sixth-grade members (the rest of us are eighth-graders).

I explained my situation. Well, almost all of it. I didn't say I felt sad and friendless, just that I needed a change of pace.

Jessi was all smiles when I mentioned tap dancing. "Stand up. I'll give you a lesson," she said.

"Now?" I asked.

"Before the others get here. Come on, hold on to the side of your desk."

I did.

"Okay, watch." She began shifting from side to side. "Ball *change*, ball *change*. . ."

I tried to copy her. It wasn't hard to do, but I looked like a real idiot.

When she started doing things called shuffles and falaps, I was hopeless.

The problem is, Jessi is practically a professional. She goes to all kinds of dance classes. (Ballet is her speciality. She's performed lead roles in productions at her ballet school.) She even looks like a dancer. She's thin and graceful, with turned-out feet.

Jessi and Mal are our junior officers. Neither of them is allowed to babysit during the evenings, unless it's for their own brothers and sisters (and they really complain about *that*), but they do a lot of sitting on afternoons and at weekends. They are absolute best friends. They are also certified horse fanatics (I think they have memorized the plot of every single *Saddle Club* book).

Like Mal, Jessi's the oldest in her family, and is convinced that her parents treat her like a baby. Unlike Mal, Jessi has a normal-sized family, with two siblings. Also, Jessi's African-American and Mal's white.

"No, no!" Jessi was saying to me. "You shift your weight on a falap. That's what makes it different from a shuffle!"

Uh-huh.

My dreams of stardom were flying out of the window.

By now, the rest of the members of the BSC had arrived. I hoped we could settle down and forget I even mentioned tap.

But no. Shannon Kilbourne and Dawn Schafer were holding on to a bookshelf and doing perfect falaps (or maybe shuffles). Kristy was trying to imitate them, but her tap dancing looked like soccer practice.

Only Mary Anne Spier had the good sense to stay sitting.

"Come on, Mary Anne," Kristy urged her.

"I, er, have to do some updating," Mary Anne replied, blushing. She was holding the BSC record book in front of her, like a shield.

Mary Anne blushes a lot. She's the shyest, sweetest, most sensitive person on earth. Also the most organized. Which makes her a perfect club secretary. You should see that record book. In her neat handwriting, she fills a calendar with all our jobs and conflicts (doctor's and dentist's appointments, family trips, Kristy's practices, Jessi's dance classes, and so on). She also keeps an up-to-date client list, with addresses, phone numbers, rates charged, and special needs, likes and dislikes of the kids we sit for. And, believe it or not, she *enjoys* doing this!

Like Kristy, Mary Anne used to live in my road. You'd never think those two opposites would be best friends, but they are. Actually, they do have things in common. Both are short and brown-haired. And they both had pretty sad lives that changed for the better.

Mary Anne's mum died when Mary Anne was a baby. Her dad brought her up by himself, and he went overboard with rules. Right through seventh grade Mary Anne had a super-early curfew, and she had to wear little-girl clothes and keep her hair in plaits.

Mr Spier began to loosen up a little in time. But things really changed when Dawn Schafer moved to town. You see, Dawn's mum used to be sweethearts with Mary Anne's dad, back when they went to Stoneybrook High School. But Dawn's grandparents thought he was too low-class or something, so the romance ended. Dawn's mum moved to California, married a man called Jack Schafer, had Dawn and her younger brother, divorced her husband, and came back to Stoneybrook. By that time, Mrs Schafer had forgotten about her old boyfriend Richard Spier. Then Dawn became close to Mary Anne, and together they found out about their parents' long-ago romance. So . . . Dawn and Mary Anne matched them up again. And we all cried at the wedding.

Mary Anne and her dad moved into the Schafers' farmhouse, which is two hundred years old and extremely cool. Now the Schafer/Spiers are one big, happy family.

Sort of.

Dawn's brother, Jeff, hated Stoneybrook. From the moment he moved here, he was miserable and homesick. Eventually Mrs Schafer let him move back to California to live with his dad, and he's been much happier.

Recently Dawn became homesick, too. So *she* went back to California, but only for a few months. (During that time her dad remarried, and Kristy, Mary Anne and I went to the wedding.)

Dawn and I are *so* different. Physically, for one thing. Her hair is practically white, and she has pale, freckled skin. Another big difference is our taste in food. Now, I have nothing against healthy eating. Seriously. I do eat unjunky food. But I just don't understand how anyone could get excited about tofu. (Have you ever tasted the stuff? It's like eating warm socks.)

Dawn can get excited about it, though. She also gets excited about non-food things such as global warming, ozone layers, rain forests and animal testing. She is such an independent thinker. She doesn't care what anyone else thinks of her.

As alternate officer, Dawn takes over whenever another member is absent. Recently she's been our treasurer, ever since Stacey left the BSC.

Which brings me to the story of Stacey.

Okay. First of all, Stacey is (or *was*) a very cool girl, and one of the original BSC members. She has gorgeous golden-blonde hair, and an incredible sense of style—sophisticated and urban, and up-to-the-second. She was born and brought up in New York City, and she often visits her dad there (the McGills are divorced).

Anyway, Stacey recently met this guy, Robert Brewster, who's good looking, athletic, clever and sensitive. He's also in LUV with her. So, naturally, Stacey began spending a lot of time with him and his friends. But then she started arriving late to BSC meetings. And backing out of jobs. And acting superior to other BSC members. And not inviting club members to a party at her house (*I* was the only one invited, which made me feel weird).

Then came the Big Fight. Everyone blew up at Stace during a BSC meeting (and vice versa). She resigned and Kristy fired her at the same time.

I was pretty angry with Stacey then. I still don't go around with her, but I've calmed down. I've started saying hi to her at school. (The other club members don't, which I think is rather immature.)

I wish Stacey had never met Robert. I have nothing against him. Or against her. It's just the situation. I miss Stacey, especially at our meetings. I could picture her that Wednesday, trying to tap dance. She'd probably be just as clumsy as the rest of us, but she'd look great.

"Er, listen everyone," I said to the thundering herd. "I don't think I'm cut out for this."

"No, you're fine!" Jessi insisted.

But before Jessi could show me another way to look like a clot, my clock radio clicked to five-thirty.

"Okay, enough," Kristy harrumphed. "This meeting of the Babysitters Club will come to order!"

Panting for breath, we all sat down.

"The first order of business," Kristy said, "is Claudia's problem. Okay. You've had a tap lesson. Now, Shannon and I would be happy to give you a drama lesson."

Drama lesson?

"Hang on!" I protested. "Can't we just, like, talk about it?"

"You bet," Kristy replied. "Shannon, you have the floor first."

Thank you, Kristy Thomas, talk-show host.

Shannon, by the way, is one of our two associate members (the other is Logan). Associates aren't required to attend meetings, but Shannon's been helping out since Stacey left. Shannon goes to a private school called Stoneybrook Day. (The rest of us go to Stoneybrook Middle School.) She's in tons of extracurricular activities there, including drama club.

"Well, we've started *You Can't Take It With You*," Shannon said. "At the moment we're just blocking, though."

"Not the football kind," Kristy remarked.

"No. Blocking is mapping out all the movements. Entrances, exits. Stuff like that has to be precise. I's like choreography, sort of."

"I remember seeing some of that in *Peter Pan* rehearsals. Is it difficult?" I asked.

"A little. All your moves happen on specific lines of the dialogue. You mark down all the moves in your script. You memorize your cue lines. Then, after you've memorized your own lines, you've memorized the blocking, too."

Right. Sure. Gosh, that sounded easy.

I might as well join the maths club.

"What happens if you forget your lines during a performance?" I asked.

Shannon smiled. "That's called 'going up'. The actor's nightmare. Happens to everybody."

Oh, yeah? Well, not to me.

My list was no use. Nought out of six.

The rest of the meeting was pretty busy with phone calls. We didn't talk much more about my problem. Which was okay. I didn't want to make it seem like a big deal.

Calm down, Kishi, I told myself. Life wasn't so bad.

Just dull.

I said goodbye to everyone, then flopped on to my bed. In about ten minutes, I'd have to start helping with dinner. Not enough time for homework, and I didn't feel in an artistic mood.

I flicked on my clock radio. It was tuned, as always, to the local radio station, WSTO. A rock song was playing, and I listened to the end of it. My eyes started feeling heavy. I could feel myself dozing off.

"And that was U4Me, rockin' it for you here on WSTO!" chirped this goony-sounding deejay. "We'll have more music for you in a minute, but first let me tell you about our *cooooool connnntesssssst. . .*"

Those last two words were full of echo or reverb or whatever they call that. It was giving me a headache. I reached out to turn the radio off.

"Say, kids, if you've been listening to me and thinking, 'Hey, I could do that,' well, here's your chance. *You* can be the host of your own show on WSTO. A kids' show. That's right. If you're between the ages of ten and fourteen—that's years, ha ha—you can have your own one-hour radio show, twice a week for . . . a fuuullll monnnnnth!"

My hand froze.

"You find the guests," he went on. "You plan and emcee the show. It's all up to you, if you're the winner of our Host of the Month Contest! To enter, just tell us why we should hire you—on one sheet of paper, please. Make it serious, make it funny, make it *you*! Don't forget to include your name, age, address and a description of yourself and your interests. We'll announce the winner on Monday, so hurry. And now, more *greaaat muuuusic*!"

My mind was racing.

My very own radio show! Me, Claudia Kishi, a deejay.

Yes. I could see it.

This was it.

This was what I was looking for!

3rd CHAPTER

I wuld like to be a kids radio show hoast becaus I have alot of expirience with kids and

Look no more. I, Claudia Kishi am exacly the person you want. You'll be sorry if you

Hi. I'm Claudia Kishi, but my freinds call me Claud. WSTO is a cool stacion. And I mean that.

The position of Hoste is of grat inportanse eppeshully considering the rabbid listeners who so intensly listen

No. No. No.

Everything sounded awful.

I dropped my pen, propped up my elbows on my desk, and buried my face in my hands.

Think, Claudia!

What had happened to me? I used to be a pretty decent writer. Seriously. When I was doing my Personal column for the *SMS Express*, I had to deal with tons of horribly written personal ads. Sometimes I'd rewrite them from scratch. First I'd decide exactly what the person was trying to say. Then I'd cut out the words that weren't necessary.

The essentials. That's what I needed.

The brilliance would come later.

I wrote out a list. Just short sentence fragments. Exactly why I wanted the job.

Then I worked on putting it all together into an essay. I tried to keep it short, sweet, and really *me*.

I consumed a Milky Way, a tube of mints, two Yorkie bars, and half a bag of crisps.

At last I had to go to sleep. My brain was fried. (My stomach didn't feel too great either.)

I worked on the essay the next morning, before I went to school. Then, during lunch, I persuaded Emily Bernstein (the *SMS Express*'s student editor) to let me use the newspaper's word processor for my final draft.

I typed my essay out carefully. Then I closed my eyes, held my breath, and prepared for the worst part.

Spellcheck.

My spelling stinks. The computer went wild. It must have stopped at a hundred misspelled words. I thought it would crash from overwork.

But when it had finished, my essay looked like this:

WHY I WANT TO BE WSTO HOST OF THE MONTH

by Claudia Kishi

Here is my idea of a great host for a kids' show:

Someone who's not shy but is also a good listener. Someone who knows what kind of music, fashion, and jokes kids like. Someone who understands the problems and concerns of kids of all ages. And most of all, someone who's reliable and hard-working.

And that someone is me, Claudia Kishi!

Okay, first of all, let me say right out, I don't have any radio experience. But I'm an

*expert at talking. Just ask any of my friends.
(On second thoughts, don't. Take my word
for it!)*

*As for reliable and hard-working? Well,
I babysit a lot. In fact, I'm vice-chairman
of a babysitters club that meets three times
a week. I also used to run a column in the
Stoneybrook Middle School newspaper,
called* Claudia's Personals.

*From my column and my babysitting, I've
learned a lot. I think I know what kids like —
from infants right on up to eighth graders!*

*I once heard an old saying that went,
"Having an open mind is one thing, but
letting bats fly around inside it is something
else entirely." Well, my mind is open to the
experience of a radio show. But the only
things flying around inside it are my ideas
for programming. I can't wait to share them
with you!*

Not bad, huh? Serious but humorous, not
too formal, well-spelled. And it's always
nice to throw in a little quotation. (I'd
been dying to use that one. I read it in a
book once, and I think it is so cool.)

"Good afternoon, this is Claudia Kishi
on WSTO," I said as I pressed the print
key.

Gosh! That felt so good! I started
giggling.

Then I forced myself to stop. *Do not NOT NOT get your hopes up*, I thought. Probably dozens—hundreds —of kids would be entering. Kids who deejayed in summer camp. Whose parents were in the radio business. Who worked on school "radio stations" broadcast over PA systems. Who could write Pulitzer Prize-winning essays.

I had to be realistic.

One thing was sure: I did not want anyone to know about this. That way, if I won, I could surprise them all with the good news, but if I lost, I could just keep the humiliation to myself.

I took the essay out of the printer, folded it, and put it in an envelope. Before I put it in my shoulder bag, I gave it a little kiss.

"Tomorrow we expect a high in the low fifties, cooler by the Sound. . ."

It was Monday, 5:29. I was in my bedroom, together with the other members of the BSC, listening to my clock radio. Well, *I* was listening to the radio. Everyone else was chatting about I don't know what.

I was a complete nervous wreck. For five days I had not stopped thinking about my essay. I rewrote it over and over in my mind. I couldn't sleep.

And now, the Big Day had arrived. Today the winner was going to be announced.

When? On which show? I had no idea. I hadn't paid attention to that part.

Which meant I had to listen to everything.

Beeeep. "WSTO news time is five-thirty," said the announcer.

"Order!" barked Kristy.

I managed to zap myself back into reality.

Dawn held up the BSC's "treasury", a manila envelope. "Subs day!"

Everyone muttered and grunted and reached for money. (No complaining from me, though. I don't mind subs. Mainly because they help pay my phone bill.)

"And now, from the sixties," the WSTO deejay was saying, "an old, mouldy, good and goldy! Here are the Beatles with—"

"Claudia, could you turn that thing off?" Kristy said.

"I love the Beatles!" I blurted out. (Okay, I was exaggerating.)

"Since when?" Kristy asked.

"Well, er, okay, I'll turn it down." I

turned the knob (slightly) and changed the subject. "Er, anybody want Skittles?"

"Me! Me!" a chorus of voices answered.

"Yeah, yeah, yeah," the Beatles wailed.

I dug the Skittles out of my sock drawer. No one seemed to mind the song much. Soon it was business as usual—munch, chat, chat, munch. I kept quiet, my ears tuned to the radio.

The phone must have rung, because I noticed Kristy snatching up the receiver. "Hello, Babysitters Club," she said. "Okay. We'll call you right back." Then she hung up and announced, "We need two sitters for the Barrett/DeWitt kids on Saturday."

Mary Anne looked in the record book. "Let's see, Dawn's free, and so are you, Kristy."

Kristy called Mrs DeWitt back. "It'll be me and Dawn, Mrs DeWitt. . . Okay, 'bye."

Kristy hung up. The radio droned on: "We have a three-mile tailback on Route Ninety-Five. . ."

Kristy yawned. Jessi and Mal were playing Hangman on the floor. Mary Anne was scribbling in the notebook. Dawn and Shannon were looking at a magazine.

And I was listening to: ". . . allow at

least a half hour leaving Stamford to the east. . ."

Kristy reached for the radio. "This is giving me a headache."

"No, don't!" I snapped.

Rrrrrrinnnng!

Saved by the phone. I leaned over the radio, blocking Kristy, and picked up the receiver. "Hello, Babysitters Club!" I said.

"Yes, hello, dear. This is Ginger Wilder, and I was wondering if someone was free on—"

"And now we have for you the winner of our *Host of the Month contest . . . ontest . . . ontest . . .*" the announcer intoned (with *lots* of reverb).

"Aaaargh! Mrs Wilder, can I call you back?" I said.

"Oh, my. Is something wrong?" Mrs Wilder asked.

"About five minutes, Okay? Sorry!"

"Fine. I'll be h—"

Click.

I hung up. I cannot believe how rude I was. Around me were six dropped jaws and twelve bewildered eyes.

I turned up the radio. "We have read them all," the announcer said. "And they were terrrrrific! But we believe we have a winner. The first place essay for the

WSTO *Ho-o-o-o-st* of the Month contest was written by. . ."

A drumroll began. I wanted to die. I was sitting there with my stomach inside out, and they were playing a *drumroll*!

"Would you mind telling us what is going on here?" Kristy said testily.

"Sssshhhh!" I hissed.

"Claaaaaaaaudia Kishiiiiiiii!" blared the announcer.

I did not react. I did not even smile. I couldn't. My body had frozen and my heart had stopped.

No. It was a joke. He was kidding. Or he was wrong. He read the wrong name. That had to be it.

"Claudia is an eighth-grader at Stoneybrook Middle School who likes art, reading mysteries, and fine dining. . ."

"Fine dining?" Kristy murmured.

"Aaaaaaaaaaargh!" I shrieked. "I won! I won!"

I jumped up and started falaping around the room.

Everyone else was staring at the radio as if it had suddenly grown horns.

"So, Claudia," the announcer went on, "if you're within the sound of my voice right now, please call five-five-five-WSTO. To repeat, that's—"

I was already on the *W*.

The phone rang on the other end—once, twice, three times.

I thought I would faint.

I caught Mary Anne's glance. She was grinning at me. Tears were filling her eyes.

At last I heard a male voice say, "WSTO, Radio Stoneybrook."

"Huck—heck—hum. . ."

Lovely. I'd won the contest of my dreams, and a frog had jumped down my throat.

"Excuse me, could you speak louder?" the voice asked.

"I'm Caudia Klishi!" I stammered.

"Yes, what can I do for you?"

"*Claudia Kishi!* I'm Claudia Kishi! I won the Host Contest!"

"Oh! Hey, congratulations! That was some essay!"

"Thanks."

"Listen, the station manager, Mr Bullock, would like to tell you about the job in person. Say, tomorrow after school? Four-thirty or so?"

"Fine!"

He gave me directions. I grabbed the nearest pen and scribbled them down on a sweet wrapper.

After blabbering a goodbye, I calmly, quietly hung up.

"Yah-hoooo!" Kristy whooped.

The room exploded. Mary Anne and Dawn threw their arms around me. Jessi and Mal jumped up and down, squealing.

"You're a star!" Dawn said.

"How come you didn't tell us you'd entered?" Kristy asked.

"I wanted it to be a surprise!" I explained.

For the rest of the meeting we talked about nothing else. I celebrated by digging out a box of chocolate cupcakes. (We almost forgot to call Mrs Wilder back.)

I could not wait to tell my family the news.

4th CHAPTER

You know who's really, really great? My sister, Janine. I mean it.

Here's what happened when I broke the news at dinner: Mum and Dad smiled. Then Mum asked if the show would interfere with my schoolwork. Dad wanted to know if I would be paid.

Janine? She immediately ran into the kitchen. When she came back, she had a bottle of ginger ale and four wine glasses.

"A toast to Claudia, the first media celebrity in the family!" she announced.

"Hear, hear!" Dad said.

Janine was the first to clink glasses with me. She was wearing this huge grin.

I almost cried.

Between dinner and bedtime, every single BSC member called. Dawn gave me a list of songs to play (ecology-

39

oriented, of course). Kristy told me her brother, Charlie, had agreed to drive me to the radio station the next day. Then she asked about seven hundred questions about the show. Shannon, Jessi, Mal and Mary Anne each had questions of their own. I must have said "I don't know" a hundred times.

This worried me. Was I *supposed* to know? Was Mr Bullock really expecting me to come to the meeting with suggestions? Of course he was! I had written in my essay that I had good ideas flying around my brain. I had exaggerated. A lot.

Now what? Should I bring tapes to the interview? A list of talk-show-type topics? A list of people to interview? Or was this supposed to be a phone-in show?

What had I got myself into?

That night I had nightmares. The whole world was listening to WSTO. Kids riding bikes and wearing headphones. Shoppers in malls. A capacity crowd in a sports arena with enormous speakers on stage, wailing: "And now, WSTO presents what you've all been waiting for— Claudia Kishi!"

And then, dead silence.

By morning I must have sweated off ten pounds.

* * *

I sleepwalked through school the next day. After the last lesson, I walked to the front door, clutching my directions to the station.

Kristy was waiting for me there. Mary Anne and Dawn joined us soon after.

"Your hairslide is crooked," Dawn said, reaching towards my hair.

"This is exciting!" Mary Anne said, squeezing my hand.

"I'll go in with you if you want," Kristy volunteered.

"Er, I don't think so, Kristy," I said.

"Keep still!" Dawn warned.

"Listen, everyone, it's not that big a deal!" I insisted.

HONK! HONK!

Saved by the Junk Bucket.

That's the name of Charlie Thomas's car, for exactly the kinds of reasons you'd expect. It is air-conditioned by two holes in the floor. You have to open the right front window with a monkey wrench. The rear floor is carpeted with crushed Coke cans.

Kristy opened the back door, picked up an old T-shirt from the floor, and wiped off the seat. "Enter," she said.

"Good luck!" Mary Anne and Dawn shouted.

I climbed in the back and Kristy got in the front. "Thanks," I called out of the window.

"I'll take good care of her," Kristy assured them. Then she yelled to a group of kids standing in front of the car: "Clear, please! Radio star coming through."

Bang! Clank! Rrrrroar! The Junk Bucket's noise was enough to scatter everybody.

We were off.

"Where to?" Charlie asked.

I read him the directions, and he clanked away from the school. His radio was turned up so loud, I expected the police to pull us over. The station? WSTO, of course.

"You ain't nothin' but a hound dog," sang the voice of Elvis Presley.

"Don't they play any *good* stuff?" Charlie asked.

"They will on *Claud's* show," Kristy replied confidently. "Right, Claud?"

"I suppose so," I said.

"Not to mention the guest appearances," Kristy banged on. "You will have kid guest appearances, right?"

"Well, I don't know."

"Or, like, a comedy hour," Charlie chimed in. "I've memorized this Robin Williams routine and—"

"*Hour?*" Kristy shot back. "Don't be a hog, Charlie."

I sighed. Already this show was overwhelming me.

The radio station was on the outskirts of Stoneybrook, in a low brick building near the highway. Two tall towers stood next to it, with blinking lights on top. The Junk Bucket chugged noisily into the car park.

While Charlie waited in the car, Kristy walked inside with me to a small reception area. A young man was sitting at a desk, wearing a telephone headset and sipping coffee. His desk was piled with memos. On the walls around him hung photographs and plaques.

"Claudia?" he said, looking up.

"Yes," Kristy answered.

"Hi. My name's Max. I spoke to you on the phone—"

"I'm Kristy Thomas," Kristy said with a big grin, reaching out to shake the guy's hand.

He gave her a puzzled look. "You're the assistant?" he asked.

Kristy's eyes lit up. "Yes!"

"No!" I exclaimed.

All three of us laughed. I gave Kristy a sharp nudge in the ribs.

Max pressed a button on his telephone

console and said, "The first-place girl is here, Mr Bullock." Then he said to me, "He'll be out in a second. Have a seat."

Almost immediately a tall, thin, grey-haired man with glasses and a great smile walked into the room.

Kristy bounced to her feet.

"Claudia, this is Mr Bullock," Max said.

Mr Bullock energetically shook Kristy's hand. "Hello, there, Claudia! Congratulations!"

"Er, Mr Bullock," I said meekly, standing up, "*I'm* Claudia."

Mr Bullock looked confused.

Ugh! What a great start!

I gave Kristy a Look. "This is my friend, Kristy. She'll be waiting outside to take me back."

"Great," Mr Bullock said. He gave Kristy a friendly wink, then turned to me. "Okay, this way, Claudia."

I could feel Kristy's eyes burning a hole in the back of my head as Mr Bullock led me down a corridor.

We passed three doors, marked *Studio* 1, *Studio* 2, and *Studio* 3. Through two of them I could hear muffled sounds of music. The floors were thickly carpeted, and so were the walls (soundproofing, I suppose). At the end of the corridor were two other doors, the one on the left marked *Conference Room* and the one on the right, *Station Manager*.

"My office," Mr Bullock said, opening the door on the right. "Believe it or not, it's highly organized."

I tried not to laugh. The place was a pigsty. It looked sort of like my bedroom. I sat on a chair that was empty (probably just cleared for the occasion).

As Mr Bullock began to close the door, I heard Max call out, "Mr Bullock, the other girl's here."

Other girl?

"Terrific," Mr Bullock said. "Send her in." He stood at the door, smiling. "Here's your assistant, Claudia."

"Assistant?"

Mr Bullock nodded. "The second-place winner gets to assist you. Competition rules. And believe me, you'll be glad you have one. A radio show is hard work."

From my seat I could not see who was approaching. "Hello, there," Mr Bullock said into the corridor. "Welcome to WSTO, and congratulations."

As my assistant walked through the doorway, I froze.

Ashley Wyeth was shaking hands with Mr Bullock.

Ashley Wyeth, the Artist with a capital A. Ashley Wyeth, who moved to Stoneybrook from Chicago, where she had studied at the country's best art school. Who wore peasant dresses and combat boots and had six ear holes. Who liked my artwork and became my friend—then told me I should leave the BSC and devote my life to "my calling". Who almost single-handedly turned all my best friends against me.

Needless to say, Ashley and I did not stay friends. Not that we became enemies or anything (although the BSC members couldn't stand her). I just realized that an artist, especially a kid artist, had to have a life.

Ashley was the last person I'd have expected to see at WSTO. Why on earth had she gone in for *this* competition? Did she want old wax records to melt for a sculpture? Was she interested in sketching a microphone?

And why was she wearing ordinary clothes? Her outfit was a plain, buttondown shirt and khaki slacks with running shoes. (She still had six studs in her ears, but I suppose you can't plug up the holes, can you?)

"Claudia Kishi," Mr Bullock said. "This is Ashley Wyeth."

46

Ashley smiled. "Hi, Claud. How's your art?"

"Great," I replied. "Yours?"

"Fine."

"So you know each other," Mr Bullock said. "That's terrific."

I forced the sides of my mouth upwards into a smile.

Mr Bullock cleared off another chair, and Ashley and I sat. "Now, I want you to know how thrilled we are to have you two aboard," he said, sitting behind the desk. "As you know, your show will be twice weekly, Thursday and Saturday, for a month. The first show will be a week from this Thursday. You'll be planning and broadcasting the shows. How you two divide your duties is completely up to you. We've never done anything quite like this, so we'll be counting on you for ideas."

Gulp!

"Do you want a music show?" Ashley asked. "Or phone-ins and featured guests?"

"Yes." Mr Bullock laughed. "In other words, anything goes. It's your show. We have facilities for all of the above. I'll just ask that you submit a programme sheet on the day of the first show, and at least a day in advance for subsequent shows. Remember, the station is at your disposal.

47

And I've assigned one of our trainees to help you. His name is Bob Atkinson, and he did a show like this in New York when he was a teenager. Okay?"

"Okay," I squeaked.

"Now, come on, let me show you around."

Mr Bullock led us back into the corridor. He pushed open the incredibly thick, padded door to Studio 1. Outside the door was a red light that said *On Air*. It was unlit.

Inside was a room with electronic equipment crammed in every corner. Shelves of tapes and CDs lined the walls and a rock song was playing loudly.

One wall was glass, from about waist up. Through it I could see a man sitting at a desk. He was young and skinny, and his hair was in a ponytail. He was wearing earphones, bopping along with the song, and scribbling something on a sheet of paper.

"That's one of our engineers, testing the equipment," Mr Bullock said with a smile. "You'll be sitting in this big room with your guests, and the technical staff will work behind the soundproof glass."

Wow! I was beginning to tingle. I could not wait to start.

Ashley was beaming, too.

The engineer caught a glimpse of us and waved his pencil. I waved back.

Mr Bullock took us to a huge stock-room with nothing but shelves of records, tapes and CDs. "Our library," he called it.

Next we saw the conference room. In there, a bearded, dark-blond-haired guy was putting labels on tapes and eating a doughnut.

"Bob, meet Claudia and Ashley," Mr Bullock said.

"Hey, the two winners!" he said, offering his hand. "Nice to meet you. Has Mr Bullock managed to scare the living daylights out of you yet?"

Ashley and I laughed. Neither one of us dared to say yes.

"Well, I'll leave you three," Mr Bullock said. "Come and talk to me if you have any questions."

We said goodbye, and Bob pulled up a couple of folding chairs for us. I got three cups of water from a water cooler in the corner. From under the piles of tapes, Bob pulled out an A4 pad.

"Your first dangerous mission, should you accept it," he said, "will be finding two things: a title and a format. By format, I mean, how exactly are you going to divide up the hour? What kinds of features? How long? Will they be continuing? Varying from show to show? Stuff like that."

Nod, nod, nod, nodded Ashley and I.

"At some point, you'll want to look at these notes," he said, pushing the pad towards us. "Just some stuff I did in New York. Like ... 'Mr Science', a phone-in show on which kids learn weird science facts from this wise-cracking, street-smart character. Kids loved that. Then we had 'Book Talk'. Kids reviewed books and actually spoke to their favourite authors. You got the idea." He looked at his watch. "Now, I have a few things I need to do. Talk among yourselves. I'll be back."

He rose from his seat, shot out of the door, and closed it behind him.

I was alone in the room with Ashley Wyeth.

Suddenly I wished I had decided on the tuba, after all.

"I, er, didn't know you were interested in radio," I said, trying to be friendly.

Ashley shrugged. "The competition sounded fun. It was sort of, you know, spur of the moment."

"But won't this take time away from your art?" I asked.

"I suppose so. But art isn't everything."

I laughed. "I never thought I'd hear *you* say that."

"Yes. I suppose not. Well, people change, don't they?"

"Mm-hm. Yes. I suppose so."

Ashley pulled the pad close to her. "Okay, let's see. . ." she said. "We can definitely do without this 'Mr Science' thing."

"Oh. I liked that idea."

"Are you serious?" She raised her eyebrows. "Well, you're the boss, aren't you?"

I did not like her tone of voice, but I let it pass. Instead I leaned over and read, "'Tom the Taxi Driver'—special guest who answers kids' questions about feelings and behavioural issues." I burst out laughing. "No!"

"Really? I think that sounds perfect," Ashley said.

Slowly but surely, my heart was starting to feel like the *Titanic*. Sinking fast.

5th CHAPTER

"How about 'For Kids Only'?" I suggested, taking a plate from the pile in the canteen.

"I don't think we should have the word *kids* in the title." Ashley picked up a small bean sprout salad, inspected it carefully, then put it on her lunch tray. "It's kind of patronizing."

Patronizing? You patronize *places*, don't you? Restaurants and shops? I had no idea what she was talking about.

"'The Young Adults Education Hour'?" I suggested.

"Please!"

"'Yo, Dudes'?"

Ashley furrowed her brow. "It might be too informal."

"It was a joke, Ash."

I smiled. Ashley smiled. I grabbed two

bowls of chocolate pudding and walked into the lunch room.

Have you ever met anyone with absolutely no sense of humour? That's Ashley.

Our meeting at WSTO had been pretty much a disaster. We hadn't fought or anything. But we were in two different worlds. Immediately we'd forgotten Bob's instructions and started talking about features. Ashley would suggest something like "A Mozart Moment" or "Art Gallery Calendar", and I'd pretend to consider it. Then I'd come up with "Stoneybrook Top 40" or "Guest Film Review", and she'd kind of snort and sniff and say, "Well, you're the boss."

So I had to humour her stupid ideas, and feel bad about mine.

Then Bob had come back to the conference room and reminded us to concentrate on a title and format. He'd suggested we meet him the next day with some "concrete ideas".

And here we were, the next day, and our concrete ideas were still in the mush stage.

"'Something for Everyone'," Ashley said as she sat at a table.

"Nice," I lied. "But that name could be for anything. Kids should hear the title and know what the show's about straight away."

Ashley scowled and fed herself a mound of bean sprouts.

I didn't want to spend the whole day bickering about the title. So I decided to change the subject.

I pulled a pen and A4 pad out of my shoulder bag and put them on the table. On the top page of the pad, in big letters, I had written *Format?* Underneath were notes I had taken.

"I was thinking", I said, "that maybe we should divide the show into three parts—"

"But what about a title?" Ashley insisted.

"We'll go back to that!"

"Okay. You're the—"

"What about making the first part music?" I suggested. "That'll get us off to a good start."

Ashley frowned. "I don't know. You can hear music on any station. I was thinking of having a feature, like current events or something school-related."

Bo-ring! "What about a phone-in part?" I suggested.

Ashley thought about that for a moment. "Yes, but you know some kids. They'll phone in and act stupid."

"Yes. The Alan Gray factor," I said. Alan once came to an art show of mine and put wadded-up chewing-gum all over the floor. He would definitely call the radio show just to burp—or something worse. Still, it might work.

"What about themes?" Ashley asked. "Like, a theme for each show? And all the parts can have something to do with it?"

A great idea from Ashley! I almost choked on my food. "Uh-huh," I mumbled.

"We can play music related to the theme, interview people, maybe find some archival radio tapes."

Archival radio tapes? *Please!* "Er, why not just have kid guests, I mean, guests of our own age? You know, hold auditions, have people sing, read aloud, tell stories, whatever."

"Well, that could be part of it."

Now I could see Kristy and Mary Anne coming our way. Mary Anne was eyeing us with caution. Kristy was more obvious. She looked completely disgusted.

Ashley, as I mentioned, is not beloved by the BSC.

"Oh, *Ashley!*" Kristy said, with the same tone of voice she might have used if she'd found Godzilla sitting next to me.

"Hi," Ashley replied.

"Ash is my assistant on the show," I quickly explained to Mary Anne. I had told Kristy about her on the way home from WSTO.

"You're doing an art show?" Mary Anne asked.

I explained carefully. I wanted to make sure Kristy and Mary Anne knew that Ashley wasn't up to her old tricks again.

I think it worked. My friends sat with us and ate peacefully.

Well, at least Mary Anne did. Ashley and I had to put up with Kristy's constant questions. But by the end of the lunch period, I had written down our tentative format:

FOUR KIDS ONLY (working titel)
1. Themes — one for each show, like:
"Frenship," or something to do with a
holiday or seasin, like that
2. 4 seggments of 15 minits each.
3. Possible segements:
  — Kid geusts, singing, telling storys, etc.
  etc. (to be picked by auditian
  — Interviews with kids book awthors if
  we can find some
  — phone-ins if posibile

When I'd finished, I passed it across to Ashley.

Kristy was still spilling out ideas. "Now, the play about babysitting will not only be educational, but a good advertisement for us—"

"Hang on!" I said. "Not so fast, Kristy. You're not on the show yet."

"I'm not?"

"Well, no. I mean, we haven't had auditions."

"Piece of cake," Kristy replied. "Mary Anne, you could play—"

"No," Mary Anne interrupted. "No way."

As Kristy rambled on, Ashley pulled a pen out of her rucksack.

"What's that for?" I asked.

"Your spelling," Ashley replied. "It's atrocious. And you've also used the title we rejected."

I grabbed the sheet out of her hands. "It's only a rough draft, Ashley. And it says, '*Working* Title'."

Ashley just shrugged. "Well, I suppose you don't really need my help, then."

"What do you mean?"

"You and Kristy seem to have the whole thing worked out."

"You just called Claudia atrocious!" Kristy snapped.

57

"Not *her*—her spelling," Ashley replied.

"It's still not very nice," Mary Anne said quietly.

"Mm-hm. Okay. Well, *excuse* me." Ashley sniffed. "I was just trying to help."

"Yes?" Kristy muttered. "Well, try a little harder next time."

"What?" Ashley said.

"Never mind."

Ugh! This was not getting any better.

I wasn't optimistic as Mrs Wyeth drove us to WSTO after school. Ashley and I were just not hitting it off.

Bob was ready for us. He brought Ashley and me into the conference room and read my list (which I had typed and Spellchecked on the *Express* computer).

"Excellent!" was his first comment. (Hurrah!)

Next, he played some tapes of old shows he had worked on. In one of them, two kid hosts interviewed the author of a book called *I Hate English*, about a Chinese immigrant girl's trouble learning the English language. Then a panel of kids—some immigrants, some American-born—discussed the book. The show was incredible. I could have listened for hours.

Then we heard a phone-in show about a book that some parents were trying to ban from a school library. Bob said that as a result of the show, the book was kept on the shelves.

A quiz show, book readings by guest actors, a comedy act . . . the tape was full of great stuff.

By the end of the tape I'd filled two pages with atrociously spelled notes.

"How do we get authors on the show?" I asked.

"Phone or write to their publishing company for information," Bob replied.

Scribble, scribble, scribble.

"What about auditions?" Ashley asked. "You know for people our age?"

"We can put an ad in the *SMS Express*," I suggested.

"And we'll do regular announcements on the air," Bob said. "You can hold the auditions in the studio. We'll arrange everything. Just remember one thing."

"What's that?" I asked.

Bob laughed. "Don't book anything that'll cost us anything. Remember why you two are here."

Ash and I looked at him blankly. "What do you mean?" I asked.

"Didn't Mr Bullock tell you? About our financial state?"

Ash and I glanced at each other and shrugged. "No," she said.

"Well, one of our sponsors has backed out," Bob explained. "One that funded a lot of shows, including the show that's in your time slot. So . . . no sponsor, no money. The station had to fire a deejay and some of our staff. I'm amazed they kept me."

"The station's not going to close down or anything, is it?" I asked.

"Not yet. But it doesn't look too great."

"And that's why you had the competition?" Ashley said. "To get two unpaid staff members?"

"Well, I wouldn't put it so bluntly," Bob replied. "I mean, that was a consideration. But the station really believes in this concept. I believe in it. And I think you two are going to be fantastic!"

After our meeting with Bob, Ash was furious. As we waited outside for her mum, I could practically see the storm clouds gathering over her head. "I can't believe they're using us like this," she grumbled.

"Oh, Ash, what's the difference?" I said. "We're doing this for the experience, right? We're going to run a radio show.

Who cares about that other stuff?"

Ashley grunted. I think she agreed with me. She just didn't want to admit it.

6th CHAPTER

Saturday

I'm sorry. I'm sorry. I'm sorry.

I tried to stop her, Claudia. Honestly I did. But it was no use.

Uh, excuse me, Dawn? I object!

What I meant to say, Kristy, was that your incredible creativity was so overwhelming at the Barrett/DeWitts today, that it made my head spin.

That's better.

Kristy was really determined to be on my show. I'd only seen her like this once before, when she'd tried to persuade a TV news team to interview the BSC members. (Why? Because the baby-sitting club *Dawn* had joined when she was in California had been on TV out there.)

Each day she seemed to have a new idea. On Wednesday she suggested running radio ads for the BSC (I'd open each show saying "'For Kids Only' sponsored by the Babysitters Club"!). On Thursday she proposed a regular feature called "Thomas's Sitting Tips". On Friday it was the "Krusher Scouting Report".

I thought she'd take a break over the weekend.

I was wrong.

On Saturday, Kristy and Dawn were scheduled to sit for the seven Barrett/DeWitt kids. (Four of them are from Mr DeWitt's first marriage, and three of them from Mrs Barrett's.) By the time Dawn arrived, Kristy was already putting two things on the picnic table in the back garden. One was a baby monitor (Marnie Barrett and Ryan DeWitt, who are both two, were having a nap in the bedroom they share). The other thing was a cassette recorder.

"Hi!" Dawn said. "What's the machine for?"

Before Dawn could reply, Mr and Mrs DeWitt bustled out of the back door and said their goodbyes.

"'Bye!" yelled all the non-napping kids, who were playing statues: Buddy Barrett and Lindsey DeWitt (who are eight), Taylor DeWitt (six), Suzi Barrett (five) and Madeleine DeWitt (four).

As the grown-ups walked towards their car, Kristy cupped her hands and called out: "Okay, how many of you lot want to audition for a radio show?"

"*Meeeeee!*"

Forget statues. The five of them charged towards the picnic table.

Dawn rolled her eyes. "Claudia is going to kill you, Kristy."

Kristy laughed. "Never! Too many witnesses. Besides, we're just auditioning."

"Can I be the announcer?" Buddy cried out.

"No announcer," Kristy said. "This is a play, with parts for everybody."

"Hurrah!" the kids screamed.

"Can we do Robin Hood?" Taylor asked. "I'm Robin!"

"I'm the Sheriff!" Suzi called out.

"You're a *girl*," Buddy sneered.

"So?"

"So who am I supposed to play, Maid Marion?"

Lindsey shrieked with laughter. "Buddy's Maid Marion, Buddy's Maid Marion."

"Heyyyyy—"

Phweeet!

Kristy is the only girl I know who owns a referee's whistle. She take it with her on babysitting jobs sometimes. It makes one of the loudest noises I have ever heard. I don't know why Marnie and Ryan didn't start shrieking from inside.

Outside, the kids quietened down.

"Okay, our show is called 'Tales of Babysitting'," Kristy said. "We all play ourselves."

"Ourselves? That's no fun," Taylor complained.

"You just think so because you have the worst part in the show," Lindsey said.

"Hey!" Taylor protested.

"Be nice, you lot," Kristy said. "We have to work together. Now, our first episode is called, 'A Messy Problem', Dawn, you and I arrive at the house to see muddy footsteps on the carpet. You say, 'Hello, is anybody at home? Oh, wow, Kristy, look at those footsteps!' Okay? Got that?"

Dawn laughed. "Kristy, I can't—"

"Say it," Kristy urged her.

"Um, hello is anybody—this is ridiculous—"

"Come on, Dawn," Kristy said. "Don't ruin the show."

"Yeah!" Buddy piped up.

"Oh-wow-look-at-those-footsteps," Dawn mumbled.

"Needs a little work, but not a bad start," Kristy said. "Now, Suzi, can you do a good scream?"

"*EEEEEEEEEEAAAAAGGHH!*"

The kids thought this was hysterical. They all started screaming, too.

Dawn claimed she lost some hearing in her left ear.

"Stop!" Kristy bellowed. "Now it's my line." She let out a fake-sounding gasp. Then, in a weird, overeager voice. "Oh, SUZI! What has HAPPENED? YOU have MUD all OVER your FACE, hands and SHIRT!"

Suzi looked very concerned. "Have I?"

"It's a play, dummy," Buddy taunted.

"I'm not a—"

"Now, Dawn, say, 'Gosh, Suzi! What happened?'" Kristy directed.

"Why—I don't—oh, okay." Dawn repeated the words in a monotone.

Kristy turned to Suzi. "Now *you* say your brother was playing in the mud and

66

he came inside and smeared you with it."

Suzi squealed with laughter. "Muddy Buddy, muddy Buddy," she sang.

"Why am I the bad guy?" Buddy protested.

"*I'll* be the bad guy!" Taylor volunteered.

"That figures," Lindsey said.

"Watch it," Kristy warned.

"Oh, Kristy, what's the point?" Dawn asked.

Kristy sighed with exasperation. "The point is for listeners to hear about effective babysitting techniques, but in story form. That makes it more interesting. And the tape is so we can listen to ourselves and fine-tune the acting. Okay?"

"Yes, Kristy," Dawn said.

"Now, my turn," Kristy blundered on. "Oh DEAR, Suzi, that is NOT acceptable BEHAVIOUR, IS it? Oh, DAWN? Will you PLEASE go upSTAIRS and see where the OTHER children are and TELL them in a GENTLE but FIRM way that whoEVER brought the mud in must BEAR THE RESPONSIBILITY for cleaning it up? With our SUPER-VISION, of COURSE.'"

"You've got to be joking," Dawn muttered.

Kristy slapped her hands rhythmically

on the picnic table. "These'll be your footsteps going upstairs. Now, once you're up there, you see Buddy lying on his bed in muddy clothes, and Taylor and Lindsey—"

"I'm not stupid enough to do *that*!" Buddy said.

"It's make-believe," Lindsey retorted.

"Do we use our real names?"

"*Waaaaaaaaaahhhhh!*" squawked the baby monitor.

Dawn had never been so happy to hear a screaming toddler.

"It's Ryan. I'll go!" Dawn bolted from the table and flew inside. As she walked into the bedroom, Ryan was rubbing his eyes and whining. Marnie was still fast asleep.

"Hi, sweetheart," Dawn said, picking Ryan up. "Bad dream?"

Ryan nuzzled his face into Dawn's shoulder. She brought him into the kitchen. Through the window she heard Buddy's voice:

"Yes-you-are-right-Kristy-I-will-never-do-that-again." He sounded as if he were speaking English for the first time.

"THAT'S okay, Buddy. Heh heh! Kids will be kids," replied Kristy in her radio voice. "And did YOU get the MARKER stains off the WALL, Taylor?"

"Why are you talking so weird, Kristy?" Taylor asked.

Dawn couldn't help giggling. Ryan started giggling, too.

"Dawn?" Kristy called out.

Uh-oh!

"In here!" Dawn replied.

"Can you help us a little?"

With Ryan on one arm, Dawn trudged outside.

I was at Ash's house that afternoon, for a planning meeting. When I got home, my answering machine was flashing. The message was from Kristy.

"Claud. Guess what? I have the most fantastic idea for a regular feature. You will laugh your head off. It is so perfect. Call me soon so I can arrange an audition. Otherwise, I may submit it to another station. Okay, 'bye."

Another station? *Please.*

Auditions were going to begin on Monday. I hoped desperately that Kristy's plan was good.

7th CHAPTER

"A whole newwww worrrrrrld. . ."

Ashley and I listened patiently as a little girl with braided hair sang meekly along with the soundtrack of *Aladdin*. Her mum sat a few metres behind her, grinning at us.

Ashley casually wrote something on the A4 pad in front of her. She slid it to me and I read it.

HOW MANY TIMES HAVE WE HEARD THIS?

Just as nonchalantly, I wrote

for.

Ashley looked puzzled. I realized I'd goofed, so I grabbed the sheet back and quickly wrote an *E* after the *R*.

70

It was Monday afternoon, about four-thirty. We were sitting in the WSTO conference room, listening to auditions.

Lots of auditions.

The waiting room was packed with nervous kids and parents. Some had to wait outside in the car park.

They were lining up—for *my* show!

I felt like a Hollywood director.

How had we become so popular? The power of advertising. During the week, Ash and I had put up some posters around town. Bob had announced the auditions regularly on the air, just as he'd said he would. By Friday, kids were stopping me in the school corridors to ask questions.

Bob had called me on Sunday to say that every single audition slot had been filled. That's one every six minutes, for an hour and a half on Monday and two and a half hours on Tuesday. *Forty* people were auditioning. He had also started a waiting list, which had grown to twelve names.

"You two are the hottest thing in town!" Bob had said over the phone.

My response? Something like, "Eeeeeeeee!"

Then I'd called Ashley. She'd said, "Indeed? What pleasant news."

Just kidding. Her response had been more like, "Yahhh-hooooo!"

Yes, Ashley was loosening up. (At last. Hurrah!)

Monday passed in a blur. Ash and I met after school, and her mum drove us to the station.

That was when it really sank in. The car park was full. The waiting room was full. We had to weave through all the excited kids who were signing up. They whispered excitedly behind our backs as we passed.

We ran into the conference room and burst into giggles.

"Aaaargh!" I screamed. "Can you believe this?"

Ash started doing some kind of Irish jig.

"Okay. Okay. Let's calm down," I said.

"Right." Ash took deep breaths. "Calm. Down."

Bob had put a table and two chairs at the far end of the room. On it was a sheet with typed instructions:

Remember:
• *Be fair. Keep All Auditions to the Allotted Six Minutes.*
• *Do Not Make Promises Yet. Tell*

*Everyone You'll Call on Tuesday Night,
After You've Made Your Decisions.*
• *Write Detailed Comments on Separate
Sheets. Suggestion: Rate Each Contestant
1 (Lowest) to 10 (Highest) and Compare
Scores.*

   Keep Smiling!

> *Best of Luck,*
> *Bob*

It was all stuff we'd discussed over the
weekend. But I was glad he had typed it
out. I was too nervous to remember any
of it on my own.

"Ready and smiling," Ashley said, with
this ridiculous, ear-to-ear grin.

I nearly cracked up. (I take back what
I said about Ash's sense of humour.)

Soon Bob sent in auditioner number
one, a girl called Lisa who started singing
—you've guessed it—"A Whole New
World". In some unknown key. *Q*,
maybe. Her face went bright red every
time she went for a high note. I stopped
listening to the song and started worrying
about her health.

Next, a pair of sixth-grade boys performed a comedy routine called, "Frank
and Tim Visit Broadway". It went something like this:

Frank: Hey, want to see *Tommy*?

Tim: Who's Tommy?

Frank: Right.

Tim: Tommy Wright?

Frank: No, Who's Tommy!

Tim: That's what I asked you!

Frank: Never mind. How about *Cats*?

Tim: Oh, Tommy Katz! Why didn't you tell me?

And so on. You get the idea. Actually, it was pretty funny. I gave them a score of 8.

The third auditioner was a girl who could say anything back to front instantly. She introduced herself as Nottus Haras (Sarah Sutton) and started pointing around the room, saying things like "enohporcim" and "tenibac elif". When I said, "Wow! That's amazing," she replied, "Sknaht."

I liked her. (I hoped Yelhsa did too.)

Number four sang "A Whole New World". Unfortunately she sang it all on one note.

Seven-year-old Rosie Wilder, a BSC charge who has about a million different talents, played the coolest tune on the violin. It started out as classical, then turned into a medley of TV show themes. It was terrific, I thought.

So far, so good.

Then we heard our third "Whole New World", by Linny Papadakis, another of our charges. This was the loudest rendition so far. In fact, he kind of barked the lyrics. Out of the corner of my eye, I could see Ashley cringing.

On and on we went.

A chorus of little kids sang the theme song from "Shining Time Station". They were adorable.

We had three proposals for phone-ins, all from SMS students: (1) "Bike Advice", by Pete Black and Erica Blumberg; (2) "Fashion Tips", by Sue Archer; and (3) "What's Happening This Weekend", by Cokie Mason.

And of course, the fourth "Whole New World"'er, whom I mentioned before.

Near the very end, a boy with a skull mask walked in. In a husky voice, he introduced himself as Oswald McBelch and started burping on pitch (more or less) to "Row, Row, Row Your Boat".

I thought Ashley was going to have a fit.

"Alan Gray, is that you?" I demanded.

It was. Giggling hysterically, Alan ran out of the room, almost colliding with two frightened-looking girls in party dresses.

See what I mean? He is such a goon.

Despite Alan, we had a fantastic day. Tuesday started out well, too. We saw a kazoo band and a pair of girls called Julie and Jennifer who sang this hilarious song called "Friendship", which I'd once seen on an *I Love Lucy* show. A couple of other kids proposed a film-review section like *At the Movies*, and a trio of high school kids told ghost stories, complete with spooky sound effects.

Then Kristy arrived, with the Barrett/DeWitt kids.

Luckily Dawn had bailed out of the play by this time.

"Hi, Claudia!" Suzi and Taylor cried out, running through the door.

"We have a play!" Madeleine said.

"Duh!" Buddy remarked.

Kristy was taking off her running shoes. "Okay, actors," she called out, "take your places!"

The kids wandered around, looking at the filing cabinets and framed photos on the wall. Madeleine found the water cooler and was busy trying to work it.

"Here we go," Kristy went on. "Ahem! *A Messy Problem*, a play by Kristy Thomas."

With one running shoe in each hand,

she pounded on the table top. "These are footsteps," she explained. Then she stopped pounding and called out, "HelLO, anybody HOME?"

No answer.

Knock knock knock! *"Buddy,"* she whispered.

Buddy was reading the inscription on an autographed photo. He spun around. "Oh! Er, yes. Come in. Claudia, who's the guy in the basketball uniform?"

"Budd*yyyy*, the *play*!" Suzi said.

Buddy rolled his eyes. "Come *in*, Kristy!"

"OH my GOODNESS, LOOK at the muddy FOOTPRINTS on the CARPET!"

"AAARGGGGGH!" Suzi's scream almost made me lose my lunch.

Madeleine choked on her cup of water. She began coughing and spluttering. Ashley and I bolted up from the table and ran to her.

The door flew open. Mr Bullock rushed in and asked, "Is everything all right?"

"Fine, fine," said Kristy. "It's part of my play."

"Oh. Sorry." Mr Bullock ducked out.

Well, I don't need to go into the gruesome details, except to say that Madeleine recovered but refused to participate,

Buddy kept looking at the pictures, Taylor forgot one of his lines and burst into tears, and Kristy insisted on pounding her trainers on the table every time someone in the play needed to walk.

After six minutes, clumps of mud were sprinkled all over the table, Kristy was scolding Buddy, and the play itself had hardly started.

"Er, Kristy," I said politely. "Time's up."

I expected her to argue, but she didn't. Instead she said, "Well, you get the main idea, Claud. What time will we be on?"

Ashley and I exchanged a look. "Er, we're notifying everybody tonight," I said.

"One way or the other," Ashley added.

Kristy nodded solemnly. "Right. I suppose you have to say that, don't you? Okay, see you. Come on, everyone!"

Trainers in hand, she padded out of the office, with the five Barrett/DeWitts behind her, all shouting goodbye.

That evening, Ashley and I met in my room. I opened a bag of caramel-flavoured popcorn rice cakes and a packet of jaffa cakes. We spread out our audition notes on the bed.

"Okay," I said. "The first 'Whole New World' girl?"

"Very shy." Ashley sighed. "You know, I think this rating system is so ... dehumanizing."

"I gave her a two," I said.

"Me, too."

"How about 'Frank and Tim Visit Broadway'?" I asked. "I thought they were funny."

Ashley rolled her eyes. "Bo-ring. Another two."

"I liked them. I said eight."

"Well, you're the boss."

Why did she have to say that?

"Um, how about Sarah the back-to-front talker?" I asked.

"Weird kid," Ashley said. "I can see how that would appeal to a mass audience, but I said three. You can't seriously think. . ."

I showed her the 10 I'd written on my sheet.

"No way!" Ashley said.

I thought for a moment. "Yaw!" I replied.

Ashley looked at me blankly.

"*Way*, back-to-front?" I said.

"Oh. Ha ha."

Well, by the time we had finished, we'd disagreed on about half the performers.

One that we agreed on a hundred per cent was Kristy.

The play was out.

And guess who had to tell her?

8th CHAPTER

"You *what*?"

I knew Kristy wasn't going to take rejection lightly. She was the last person I called on Tuesday night.

"Kristy," I explained patiently, "we felt the play would be a little too long, and—"

"It's exactly fifteen minutes."

"Uh-huh. But—"

"If you want, we can cut it. No problem."

"It's just that, well, some of the kids don't seem . . . ready."

Kristy took a deep breath. "Yes. I suppose they were a little rambunctious. But you are going to have more auditions, right?"

"Yes. We haven't filled up the whole month."

'All *riiight*. 'Bye!"

I could practically hear her mind working. I knew we hadn't heard the last of Kristy Thomas.

Now for the hard part.

We'd accepted about ten acts. But we could only use four of them in the first show. We also needed to choose a theme.

(We should have chosen the theme first. That would have made it easier to pick the acts. Of course, we hadn't thought of that.)

On Wednesday Ashley walked home with me from school. Before the BSC members arrived, we'd have time for a planning session.

Over snacks, of course. No sense starving while you're planning.

Ashley crunched away on some Doritos. I was eating a Rolo.

"So how do we do this theme thing?" I asked.

Ashley swallowed before speaking. "'Do this . . . theme thing'?" she repeated, as if I'd just said something in baby talk.

"Yes. Like, let's say we pick a theme. You know, fashion, or art. How do we fit in Sarah the back-to-front talker?"

"Well," Ashley said with a smile, "*I* wasn't the one who wanted to use her."

Ooh! I wanted to slap Ashley. But I didn't. I was calm and cool. She was my assistant. She didn't have to be my best friend.

"Friendship," I said. It was the first word that popped into my mind. "Like the song Julie and Jennifer sang. How about that for a theme?"

Ashley frowned. "Well, it was only one song."

"I know. But we could, like, build the show around the song. You know, have the guests talk about what friendship means to them."

"I don't know—"

"No solo acts for this show—just twos and threes. Then they can talk about their friendships."

"How it affects their artistry."

"Exactly." (In Ashley-esque terms.)

Ashley shrugged and gave me a *well, you're the boss* look.

You know what? I didn't care. I *was the boss*. And it was a good idea.

I popped another Rolo in my mouth, grabbed a pen, and looked at the list of acts we had accepted. I circled these:

Frank and Tim (comidy)
Peet and Ericka (Bike Advise)
Shinning Time stacion cartus
Bil and Katie (at the movys)
Rijena, Cathy, David (goest storys)

"See?" I said. "All of these kids seemed like great friends. Let's choose three. We'll call them to discuss the theme. Then we'll put the friendship song last."

"One problem. The song isn't anywhere near fifteen minutes long."

"Well . . . we'll ask the girls to sing more than one song. There are plenty more songs based on friendship, right?"

"'Ben,'" Ashley replied.

"Ben who?" I asked.

"The song 'Ben'. About the boy and the rat."

"Yuck!"

"It's beautiful. It goes like this: 'Bennnnn. . .'"

Guess what? Ashley may be a great artist, but her singing is as bad as my spelling.

"Aaargh, stop!" I said. "You'll break my windows!"

Ashley's face went red. We both cracked up.

Well, by the end of our meeting, we'd decided on our big three: the comedy act, the kiddie chorus, and the film reviewers.

Ashley left at a quarter past five. I had fifteen minutes until the BSC meeting.

I picked up the phone. My first call was to Frank (of Frank and Tim). He was delighted—until I mentioned the friendship angle.

"There's one problem," he said softly. "I hate Tim."

"Oh, but I'm sure you can—"

"*Joke*! See, now *that* is comedy!"

Ugh! Maybe Ashley was right about these guys.

For the kids' chorus, I called Mrs Farrell, one of the mums who'd brought the group to the radio station. She thought the theme was a great idea, because *Shining Time Station* is all about friendship and cooperation.

Bill Sherbar, the film reviewer, seemed a little embarrassed about the theme. But he agreed to call his partner, Katie Geissinger, to discuss it.

Last, I called the two girls who'd sung "Friendship", Julie Mansfield and Jennifer Evans. They said they'd try to find two or three more songs to sing.

Phew! This was turning out to be a lot of work. But I was doing it. Me, Claudia Kishi. The artist. The girl who thinks *planning* means stocking up on Twix bars.

You know what? I was pretty proud of myself.

I could not wait until showtime.

⋆　　⋆　　⋆

85

I went out during the lunch hour on Thursday. Afterwards I put together this great new outfit and trimmed my hair.

I know. It was a radio show. Nobody was going to see me. But I could not help it. Honestly. I absolutely had to do it. I don't know why.

Anyway, I wore the coolest man's dinner jacket I'd recently bought in a charity shop, together with a silk shirt with piping and a bright red velvet cummerbund. I removed the shoulder pads from the jacket, which made it really slouchy (I love that look). Then I bought a pair of white socks with silver glitter.

I decided to wear a pair of red trainers to match the cummerbund. I swept my hair up and fastened it with a rhinestone hairslide in the shape of a musical note.

Lastly, I carefully folded up a speech I had written, typed, and Spellchecked on the *SMS Express* computer. I put it in the inside pocket of my jacket.

My dad left work early so he could drive me to the station, with WSTO turned up almost to full volume. He kept nodding his head and saying, "Nice station," even though we only heard the weather, sport, and a few ads.

He was grinning from ear to ear when

he dropped me off. "Good luck, sweetheart. We're proud of you," he said.

My dad hardly ever says that (to me, at
least). I nearly broke down. Was I glad
I'm not Mary Anne! "Thanks, Dad," I
replied. "Don't forget to tape it."

"I've bought new batteries," he called
out as he drove away.

Ashley was already in the studio when
I walked in, dressed in jeans and a
workshirt. She was deep in conversation
with Bob, but when she saw me, she
howled with laughter.

"Are you going to, like, describe your
outfit to the listeners or something?" she
asked.

"Ha ha!" I replied. "Nice to see you,
too."

I tried to look cross. At least serious.
But Ashley's face looked like Christmas
morning.

I let out a scream. She let out a scream.
We hugged each other. We jumped up
and down.

"Er . . . harrumph!" Bob said.

"Oh. Right. The show." I could hardly
speak, I was grinning so much.

We gave Bob our programme sheet.
Somehow we managed to discuss it with
him and Mr Bullock. One by one, the
guests started filtering into the waiting

room next to the studio. I think I said hi, but I don't remember. I was so nervous.

An engineer knocked on the window and pointed to the clock. It was 4:56, and the show began at 5:00.

Yikes!

Ashley and I put on our earphones (unfortunately, that meant taking off my hairslide). Mr Bullock rushed in and wished us good luck. Bob gave us a salute and sat in a corner to watch. An engineer's voice began calling out, "Ten . . . nine . . . eight . . ."

I grabbed Ashley's hand, which was clammy. She was shaking. I was shaking.

". . . Six . . . five . . ."

And I realized my speech was still in my pocket.

I let got of Ashley. I reached into my jacket with my right hand.

Wrong side. My finger caught in a rip in the lining.

". . . three . . . two . . ."

My left hand jabbed my chest. My fingers fluttered and fumbled. I had no control. My brain was somewhere in the Limbo Zone.

A red light blinked on above my head.

"You're on the air!" the voice said over the headphones.

Gulp!

The speech. It was in my hand. I had it. I smoothed it out on the table.

I could not understand a word.

"It's upside down!" Ashley whispered.

On the other side of the soundproof glass, an engineer started cracking up.

He had heard Ashley!

Quickly I turned the speech around. "Heek kew."

Oh. Oh. This was not happening. My throat was dry as dust.

I quickly swallowed. Ashley's eyes looked like white Frisbees.

"Hello and welcome to 'For Kids Only'!"

I did it! I took a deep breath and went on. "This is Claudia Kishi, coming to you live from the WSTO studios, along with Ashley Wyeth, and this is our first show. Today our theme is *friendship*."

As I continued speaking, Ashley's Frisbee's slowly shrank. When I'd finished my speech, her eyes were more or less normal-sized.

Frank and Tim performed their comedy act. But they added a new section about being friends. It consisted mostly of dumb insults, such as "With friends like you, who needs parents?" And "Tim's a

89

great buddy. I lend him my maths homework and he lets me copy his lunch."

Next the kids sang. Afterwards we asked them about the train characters of *Shining Time Station*, and then about their own experiences. They were very talkative. One little boy chattered about a pen pal in Japan. "I'm saving up to go and visit him and I already have six dollars and twenty cents!" he announced.

Bill and Katie, the film reviewers, talked about films that featured strong friendships (great idea, wasn't it?).

The only problem was that everybody was going too fast. I tried desperately to stretch out my introductions, and that helped a little.

Julie and Jennifer began their song at five-forty-two, three minutes early. (Do you know how long three minutes is, in radio time? *For ever*).

Ashley and I both signalled them to take their time (which was kind of useless, as they were singing to tapes).

First they sang the buzzard's song from the film *The Jungle Book*. Then a pop song, "That's What Friends Are For". And lastly, the song from *I Love Lucy* (which they said was written by a guy called Cole Porter). My absolute favourite line went like this:

"When other friendships have been forgot, ours will still be hot!"

They finished at five fifty-nine.

One minute left.

I looked at Ashley. Her face looked like a human question mark.

The engineer was signalling me to go on.

Dead air. That's radio talk for silence. You're not supposed to let it happen for more than a second or two.

"Um," I said. "Thank you all for listening. This is Claudia Kishi and Ashley Wyeth, with 'For Kids Only'. This has been our first show. We hope you tune in next Saturday."

Forty-three seconds were still left.

Ashley nudged me. I shrugged. That was all I'd planned to say.

You know what I was thinking?

What would Stacey do in a situation like this?

Stacey is about the coolest person I know. She'd know how to handle dead air. She'd just say what was on her mind.

I took a deep breath. "And, er, most of all, I hope you enjoyed our . . . *theme* today," I said. "Friends are really important, you know. They're like a special gift. A second family. I suppose I'm pretty lucky, because I have lots of friends, and they all live in Stoneybrook. I used to have a best friend, too, but not any more. I—I really miss her."

It felt weird admitting that over the air. But it was true.

"Anyway," I continued, "maybe she's listening right now. And if she is, I hope she liked the show."

I looked at the clock. Ten seconds left.

"So . . . we'll see you on Saturday, and don't forget: If you'd like to audition for 'For Kids Only', just call the station at 555-WSTO. That's all the time we have now. Goodnight!"

Above my head, the red light went off. Bob was beaming. "I am *so* proud of you," he said.

I screamed. Ashley screamed. Frank and Tim did a routine of strange high-fives. Bill, Katie, Julie, Jennifer and the kids were all hugging like crazy.

We mobbed Bob. He shouted for help, but no one listened.

Mr Bullock walked in with a huge smile. He laughed and laughed.

Me? I had only one regret.

I had brought absolutely no junk food in my rucksack.

9th CHAPTER

Today Kristy and I sat for my brothers
and sisters. Everything went well, except
I have a question for Claudia.

Saturday

You're not planning to extend this
radio show past one month, are you?

Can you guess why Mallory asked that question? If you think it has something to do with Kristy, you're right.

It also has to do with the Oogly Oogly Beast.

Oogly had become very popular in the Pike house. That Saturday, Claire and Margo had begged Mallory to tell them another story.

Mallory was in the middle of one when Kristy arrived.

"Hi, everyone!" Kristy called out, bounding into the playroom.

Claire glared at her. "Sssshhh!"

"Hi, Kristy!" Mallory said. "The boys are outside with Vanessa."

"Come *on*. Finish the *story*," Claire whined.

"Don't be rude," Margo warned her.

"*Pleeeeease*," Claire said, rolling her eyes.

Kristy left the room and went into the garden.

"'Who's been eating my dinner?' roared the Oogly Oogly Beast," Mallory said. "Rustylocks slowly peeped out from behind the music centre. 'I did,' she squeaked. Well, the Oogly Oogly Beast's eyes popped out. The hairs on his shoulders stood on end. Smoke poured from his ears. He gritted his teeth, flexed his claws, and stomped towards Rustylocks. 'Rrrrrragggh! You must pay for this terrible crime!' he growled. 'But what did I do?' Rustylocks asked. The Beast just roared again and drew his snarling face up to hers.''

Mallory paused. She let Claire and Margo sit there for a moment, frozen, their mouths hanging open.

'''Yoooouuu,' the Oogly snarled. 'Yooouuu neglected to put the plate into the dishwasher. Goodness me, I will simply *not* tolerate messy housekeeping!''''

Margo and Claire fell off the sofa, laughing.

And Kristy reappeared in the doorway.

"Mallory, it's perfect," she said.

"Thank you," Mal replied with a modest smile. "I—I just made it up."

"You should write it down. Really. Take my word. It'll help."

"Help what?"

"For the audition. I think that was my problem. You see, the Barrett and DeWitt kids are too young to read, but *your* brothers and sisters can."

"Except for Claire," Margo piped up.

"I can!" Claire retorted. "I know all the letters!"

"Hang on!" Mallory said. "No, Kristy.

95

The answer is no. I can't audition in front of all those people."

"You were great, Mal!" Kristy said. "You're a natural performer."

"Telling stories at home is easy. No way am I going to go on the radio!"

(Mallory, as you can guess, is a little shy.)

Kristy sat on the arm of the sofa. She looked away, thinking. "Well, what if *I* do it, then?"

"No!" Claire cried. "You can't do it like Mallory."

"How does he speak?" Kristy scrunched up her face and used a nasal voice. "'Er, excuse me, but this floor is dirty.' Like that?"

Margo giggled. "You sound really daft."

"Thank you," Kristy replied in her Oogly voice.

"Not so exaggerated," Mallory said. "Just pretend to be a really fussy person."

Mallory trained Kristy for a while. Kristy wasn't getting the voice properly, but that didn't seem to matter to her.

Kristy borrowed a notepad and pen from Mal, then ran into the garden. Mal, Claire and Margo followed closely behind her.

"Who wants to audition for Claudia's show?" Kristy called.

"Meeee!"

Round two was about to begin. This time, without a tape recorder.

Kristy sat on the grass as all seven of Mal's brothers and sisters gathered around her. "Buddy told me you've already auditioned," Nicky said, "and Claudia said no."

"Well, this'll be different," Kristy insisted. "She will crack up. We're going to do an Oogly Oogly Beast story."

"All *riiight*!" Jordan said.

"Okay," Kristy barged on, "let's say, the Oogly goes to. . ."

"Disney World!" Vanessa suggested.

"A baseball game!" Adam said.

"The toilet!" Nicky cried.

Margo groaned. "*Gross*, Nicky!"

"How about this?" Kristy said. "The Oogly Oogly Beast goes to Stoneybrook Elementary School?"

"And eats my teacher!" Byron added.

Claire sneered. "Ugh! Too messy."

Kristy began writing. She recited each word she wrote. "This . . . is . . . the . . . story . . . of . . . a . . . very . . . neat . . . monster." She laughed. "Oh, that's a good one. A neat monster. Get it?"

Mallory cringed. "Er, Kristy?"

Kristy just barged on. "The . . . monster's . . . name . . . was . . . the . . . Oogly . . . Oogly . . . Beast . . . and . . . he . . . loved . . . to . . . be . . . clean."

After a few minutes of this, Mallory had to go back inside. She couldn't take it any more. Suddenly her great creation—her very own character—seemed kind of stupid.

As she wandered into her room, she could hear her brothers and sister laughing like crazy outside.

As for me, well, I felt as if my life had been taken over by the show. (Surprised?) On Saturday night, our second one had been a little rocky. The theme had been "Family". I talked about my family, but when I mentioned Peaches and Mimi, I choked up. I almost blew my nose into the mike (*very* cool). Then our first act, a brother and sister, arrived ten minutes late because they'd had a fight. I had to swap acts around, and everyone became nervous and began fluffing their lines. And I kept speaking too close to the mike, so every time I said a word with the letter *P* I caused a small explosion.

Also, a couple of our future guests had called to cancel, so we needed to hold more auditions soon.

But the good news was that WSTO had already received some mail and calls about the show—all raves!

Mum and Dad had promised to take Janine and me out for dinner on Saturday evening. As usual, I was late getting dressed. Mum had already called me twice from downstairs. I could hear the car starting up in the drive.

Rrrrring!

Oh, great. Of all times for a phone call.

I thought about letting the answering machine take the call. But I didn't do it. Quickly I picked up the receiver. "Hello?"

"Claudia, it's me, Kristy."

"Oh, hi. Listen, I need to—"

"I think I've got it!"

"Got what?"

"An act. A great one. When can we audition?"

My heart sank.

I should have let the machine answer it.

10th CHAPTER

"Knock, knock!" said Jacki Rodowsky.

"Who's there?" I asked.

"Lena."

"Lena who?"

Jackie grinned. "Lena little closer and I'll tell you!"

Hahahahahahahahaha!

That was a laugh track. Bob was sitting with us in the conference room and fooling around with sound equipment.

We were halfway through our Tuesday auditions. The turnout was even bigger than last time, but the talent wasn't as good. (Bob said that when a show becomes popular, everybody wants to hop on board.)

Jackie was giggling so hard at the laugh track, he could barely deliver the next joke.

"Knock, knock!" he said at last.

"Who's there?" Ashley, Bob and I all asked.

"Hatch."

"Hatch who?"

"Bless you!"

Hoo hoo hee hee ho ho ho!

Bob was now playing a recording of one man bellowing with laughter. Well, Jackie laughed so hard at that, he fell off his chair.

He grabbed on to the table on his way down. Unfortunately, Ashley's and my half-filled plastic cups were on it.

The table tipped and wobbled. Cups, papers, and pens went flying off the end.

"Whoa!" Ashley yelled.

Bob bolted out of his seat to help Jackie, who had been bopped by a flying cup. "Are you okay?" he asked.

His face was red and his hair was wet. "Oops!" was all he said.

"It's my fault," Bob said. "Those laugh tracks are too distracting."

It wasn't his fault. He just doesn't know Jacki. "The Walking Disaster" is how the BSC members refer to him. Falling and spilling are two of his greatest talents. I keep hoping he'll grow out of it, but he hasn't yet.

When Ash and I had helped to clean

Jackie up, Bob thanked him for the audition and guided him safely back to the waiting room.

I sat down again and gathered my notes. Next to Jackie's name I wrote, *Cute, but where to fit?*

Ash and I had become much better at these auditions. We had decided on the themes for our next three shows in advance—"It Ain't Easy Being a Kid", "My Favourite Place in the World", and "What Are You Reading?"

"Look, we have a return customer!" Bob announced as he came back into the room.

Behind him was Kristy, clutching a few stapled-together sheets of white paper.

And behind her, also holding sheets, trudged Adam, Jordan, Byron, Vanessa, Nicky, Margo and Claire Pike.

"Claudia-silly-billy-goo-goo!" Claire called out.

"Hello, everybody, we are the Thomas-Pike players!" Kristy announced.

"Pike-Thomas," I heard Byron mutter.

Kristy read from the papers: "'Today we present the story of a very . . . *neat* monster.'" She looked at each of us and grinned, as if she'd told a joke.

Then Jordan began reading in a mumble so low I could barely hear him. "'The monna nimwa Oogelbee and he luvva be clean.'"

"Speak up!" Kristy whispered.

But before Jordan could repeat it, Vanessa shouted, "'EVERY TIME HE DID SOMETHING SCARY, HE WAS JUST UPSET ABOUT THE MESS.'"

Margo held up her sheet in front of her face.

"'Like . . . the time . . . when he . . . um, arrived home . . . and he . . . he saw Rr . . . Rrroo style—'"

"Rustylocks, you dummy!" Nicky hissed.

Margo stuck out her tongue. "'Rustylocks,'" she continued. "'And . . . he—'"

"Hey! My turn!" Adam said. "'And he said, "You ate my food but you didn't put the plate in the dishwasher."'"

Kristy laughed. "Great, Adam!"

Ashley gave me a sideways glance. She had this tense, little smile on her face.

Bob looked totally bewildered.

And I knew I was going to be making another painful phone call.

After the auditions, Ashley and I carefully pored over our lists.

"I like the kid who knew sports trivia," I said.

Ashley made a face. "I hate sport."

"I do, too. But I think kids will like him."

"Well, that's probably true."

"Do we keep him?"

"Yes. How about Jackie?"

I just gave her a Look.

She sighed. "Yes, I feel the same way."

You know what? Ashley was improving. Either that or I was being more tolerant. Whatever. The thing is, I didn't feel like strangling her every two seconds.

Maybe every two *minutes*. (Just kidding.)

A moment later Bob poked his head in the room. "Are you two hungry? I'm on my way to the snack machine to get a Milky Way or something."

I reached into my shoulder bag. "Is a Snickers okay?"

"Yes. But what about you?"

"I've got some more." I tossed him the Snickers and began rummaging through my bag. "Milk Bottles, peppermints, and I think a box of chocolate-covered raisins."

Ashley laughed. "What, no Yorkie bar?"

"Oh sorry," I said. "I ate it on the way over here."

"I'd love to be your dentist," Bob remarked, biting into the Snickers bar. He plopped himself into his chair. "Maybe that's what I should do, become a dental assistant."

"Right," Ashley said.

"I'm serious. I may need the work soon, the way things are going here."

"Uh-oh!" I said. "Are they going to fire you?"

Bob shrugged. "You know what they say: 'Last one hired, first one fired.' Mr Bullock tries to be positive about it all, but he's been dropping hints."

"What'll you do?" Ashley asked.

"I don't know. I'm only paid a small salary here, but I really need it. It goes towards my tuition fees. Maybe I'll leave college for a while."

I didn't know what to say. Neither did Ashley. He looked so sad.

Over Bob's shoulder, I noticed that the clock read 6:27. My dad was supposed to pick up Ashley and me at six-thirty. "Um, we have to go," I said.

"I'll walk you to the car park," Bob volunteered.

We gathered our stuff and began walking down the corridor towards the front door.

"I just can't imagine Stoneybrook without WSTO," I said. "I remember listening to it when I was a kid."

Bob nodded. "Me, too. And my parents heard the end of World War Two announced on WSTO when *they* were kids. Our listeners are going to be really shocked if the station goes down the drain."

"Don't they know about it?" Ashley asked.

"No," Bob replied. "The station policy has been to keep it quiet. If our advertisers find out, they'll want to desert us. No one wants to stay aboard a sinking ship."

I waved to Max and pushed the front door open. "That's stupid. If you get more people to listen, then the advertisers will want to put ads in the show. Right?"

"Yes," Bob said, holding the door for Ashley.

"So let everybody know," I went on. "The listeners care about the station. Maybe they can write to advertisers. Or donate money. Like an emergency fund."

"True," Bob said. "I mean, it's not the way things are done in commercial radio, but—"

"I think it's unfair not to tell the listeners," Ashley remarked.

"I suppose I could broadcast an editorial," Bob said. "But I'd have to get Mr Bullock's permission."

"Write an article for the *Stoneybrook*

News, too," I suggested. "That way you might reach some new listeners."

Honk! Honk!

Dad was parked in a spot at the other end of the car park. He waved at us.

"You two had better go," Bob said. "Good work."

"Will you talk to Mr Bullock about all this?" Ashley asked.

"Okay," Bob replied. "Hope springs eternal, huh?"

He smiled as we went towards the car.

But judging from the look on his face, hope was the furthest thing from his mind.

11th CHAPTER

"You *what*?"

I could not believe it. Our Thursday show was about to begin. I was in the studio, setting things up with Ashley, Bob, Mr Bullock and the engineers. And now one of our guests, Peter Hayes, was calling up to cancel.

Peter is a great athlete. He has achieved several middle-school track records. For our theme, "It Ain't Easy Being a Kid", he was going to talk about sports pressure at the state level.

"I've twisted my ankle," Peter said. "I was skateboarding."

"And you can't walk?"

"Claudia, I have to go to the doctor. Now. I mean, come *on*, I didn't do this on purpose!"

I breathed in and counted to three.

Then I breathed out and said, "I know. Sorry, Pete. Good luck. I hope you feel better soon."

"Thanks, Claud."

"No problem." I was courteous. I was polite. I was compassionate.

And then I hung up.

"*He's a track star, and he's twisted his ankle on a skateboard!*" I exploded. "*Arrrrgh!*"

"What do we do now?" Ashley asked.

"Can you do a good imitation of a track star?" Bob asked.

"Very funny," I said, pacing the floor. "How on earth are we going to fill fifteen minutes?"

"Music?" Ashley suggested.

"We can't forget the theme," I reminded her.

"Talk about the pressures of the Baby-sitters Club," Ashley suggested.

"Kristy would kill me," I said. "She'd think it was bad publicity."

The room fell silent. I could hear the equipment buzzing. The clock said 4:50. Ten minutes to showtime.

My mind was flying.

"It Ain't Easy Being a Kid". I certainly knew enough about that subject. From my home life, from my friendships, from my personal column.

That would be perfect. A personal column on the air. Well, not personal, exactly. But complaints and advice, more like Dear Abby.

"Okay, let's do a phone-in," I said. "Advice for kids."

"From us?" Ashley asked.

"Why not? We can try."

"Peer counselling," Mr Bullock said. "Good idea. I say go for it."

Ashley didn't look convinced. But she agreed. And that was all that mattered.

Rosie Wilder was the guest in our first section. She played her funny violin piece, then talked with me on-air about her conflicts. The fifteen minutes went by super-fast.

In our next two sections, we interviewed some of Ash's SMS friends she'd invited to be on the show: identical twins, and then a boy who had lived in six different places (in three countries) over the past five years.

Throughout the show, I kept saying, "And remember, our 'For Kids Only' phone-in begins at five-forty-five. Tell us what's on your mind."

An engineer had put up a huge telephone near me, with six lines. By 5:44, all six were lit up.

Ashley was sweating. She squeezed my left hand. I could feel my throat tightening. I picked up the phone and said, "'For Kids Only'. You're on the air."

"Hi, Claudia?"

"Yes?" I said. "Who am I speaking to?"

"Um, my name's Joanne. I really love your show, and I just wanted to ask you something. I had this argument with a friend, and I told her I never wanted to speak to her. But now I realize I was stupid. She hates me, but I want to be her friend again. What do I do?"

"How do you know she hates you?" I asked.

"She doesn't talk to me in school any more."

"Has either of you phoned to apologize?"

"No."

"Well, someone has to do it. Why not you? Just tell her exactly what you told me."

"But she'll hang up on me!"

"I don't believe that, Joanne. I think you need to try. I bet she'll stop being angry."

"Do you think so?"

"Yes. And good luck, Joanne."

Ashley gave me a thumbs-up.

Why, *why* did that call make me think of Stacey?

The next caller wanted to complain about a teacher. Ashley handled that one.

Caller three was a girl called Cheryl who asked, "When you're babysitting, how do you deal with a one-and-a-half-year-old boy who won't go to sleep?"

Right up my alley. "First try singing to him. If that doesn't work, pick him up and walk up and down—but keep singing. If he still won't sleep, try some warm milk with a little honey in it. If you have a rocking chair, sit in it and rock to and fro while you tell him a long story. . ."

I went through every babysitting trick in the book. Cheryl listened carefully and thanked me.

The next caller blurted out, "Why do kids have to do homework? It's the stupidest thing in the world!"

"Do you need some help with your homework?" Ashley asked.

No. He'd already done it. It turned out he just wanted to complain.

I answered a few calls. Ashley answered a few. Together we managed to give advice about hair, clothes, boys, girls, parents, grandparents, teachers, you name it. The time was racing by.

At 5:58, I announced, "Okay, I think

this'll be our last call. Hello, you're on the air."

Sniff. Sniff. "Hello?"

When I heard the sniffing, I immediately thought Mary Anne was calling. But the voice was different.

"Hi. This is Claudia."

"Hi." *Sniff.* "Um, my name's George Hewitt. I'm eleven. And ... and my parents are, well, it's like, they hate each other. They are always arguing. Now my dad hasn't been at home for a few days, and my mum says they're going to get a divorce."

I could see Ashley turning about three shades of pale. (I wasn't feeling too comfy myself. I'd sort of been hoping for a discussion about clothes or videos.)

"You sound very upset," I said.

"Well," George went on, "my mum got really angry today, and she started screaming at my little sister, Rachel. And Rachel started saying how she wished Mum would go away and Dad would come back. Then Mum started crying, and Rachel said ... well, she said she wished Mum would die, and both of them ran to their rooms. I tried to talk to them, but they told me to go away. I don't know, I—I just feel helpless. What shall I do?"

Phew! How were we going to handle

this? I looked at Ashley, but she just shook her head.

I thought about my personal column. Back then, a boy had written to me with a similar problem. I had referred him to a therapist called Dr Reese. Yes, a therapist. Mary Anne had seen her not long before, after she had become very depressed. After a few consultations, Mary Anne was on the right track again and felt much better.

I looked at the clock. It was time to wrap up.

"George, I don't think you're going to find what you need on a phone-in show," I said gently. "You need to talk to some-one professional."

"You mean, like a—"

"A therapist. Don't worry. It doesn't mean you're crazy or anything, George. It will really help. Stay on the line, okay? When we go off the air, I'll give you the phone number of someone very good."

"Okay."

I gave a little closing speech. The red light went off, and Bob came running in with a Stoneybrook phone book. I flipped through and found Dr Reese's number.

"George, are you still there?"

"Yes."

"Call Dr Reese at 555-7660, okay? Just

talk to her for a while. Tell her how you're feeling."

"Okay." I could hear the sniffling again. "Thanks, Claudia."

"Good luck, George."

Click!

When he'd hung up, I slumped back in my chair. Ashley was giving me a worried look. Bob was sipping coffee. The engineers were busily adjusting dials.

Next to Bob, Mr Bullock was leaning against a filing cabinet. "Congratulations, you two," he said. "You covered for an emergency. You worked out a suitable replacement. You've performed a valuable service."

"Thanks," I said.

"Don't thank me," Mr Bullock said with a chuckle. "Up until now, you've been doing a good show. Tonight, you became professionals."

I turned to Ashley. The colour was returning to her face.

This time, when she looked at me, I saw nothing but admiration.

Which, at that moment, was just what I needed.

12th CHAPTER

Friday

Tonight I sat for Marilyn and Carolyn Arnold. They were upset about the "twins" segment on Claud's show. They thought they should have been the ones to do it.

Boy, were they heartbroken. Devastated. I told them they shouldn't be. They hadn't even auditioned. But that didn't work. I had to think of something. I had to give them hope.

So I did . . .

Heartbroken? Devastated?

I think Kristy was going a little overboard. According to her, Carolyn and Marilyn were moping around the house that Friday afternoon. (Later, when I talked to Marilyn, she said they were reading *Jeremy Thatcher, Dragon Hatcher* to each other in the playroom and laughing out loud.)

Then Kristy found out how "upset" they were and calmed them down. (Carolyn's version was different. *She* said Kristy started talking about my show out of the blue and hinted that the Arnold twins would have made better guests than the other twins.)

Marilyn and Carolyn are eight years old. They are identical in appearance, but definitely not in personality. They used to disagree about everything. Once they actually divided their bedroom in half with masking tape. Luckily, their parents moved them into separate rooms, and now they tolerate each other much better.

Most of the time.

Anyway, I'll pick up the story of Friday a little further on—at the point where Kristy's version started matching the twins'.

"Claudia was so cool in that phone-in," Marilyn said. "That was the best show."

"Oh, boring. I liked the one about families," Carolyn volunteered.

"If I did the shows," Kristy said, "I'd have more humour in them."

"You should audition for that show, Kristy," Carolyn said. "You'd be great."

"I did," Kristy replied. "Twice. But Claudia rejected me."

Marilyn's eyes widened. "And she's your *friend*!"

"Hey, I'm not insulted," Kristy insisted. "I have more ideas. Great ones, too. If I can find a couple of helpers."

(She is so sly, isn't she?)

"How about us?" Marilyn asked.

"Yeah!" Carolyn piped up.

Bingo! Kristy was in business again. "All right. I was thinking of, 'Marilyn and Carolyn and Kristy and the Major League Mystery'. Like, we go to a ballgame and a player is missing and we have to find him."

The twins just stared at her. "That's pretty stupid," Marilyn said.

"Or maybe, 'Stoneybrook—a Tour'," Kristy blundered on. "We could talk about our favourite places, mention the library and some of the restaurants."

"Boring, boring, I am snoring," was Carolyn's criticism.

"Kristy, we have to think of something *kids* will like," Marilyn said.

"Like what?" Kristy asked.

"Dolls," Marilyn suggested.

Kristy shook her head. "That probably leaves out most of the boys."

"Good," Carolyn shot back.

"What about sport?" Kristy asked.

Carolyn made a face. "Gross. Let's do something about films."

"Someone's already doing that," Kristy said.

Carolyn thought for a moment. "I know! A game show, like *Jeopardy*."

Marilyn rolled her eyes. "Too difficult."

Kristy saw a copy of *Jeremy Thatcher* lying open on the sofa. "What about book reviews?"

The girls looked at Kristy as if she had suggested a foot-smelling competition.

"A book *reading*?" Kristy quickly suggested.

"Yeah!" cried Marilyn.

"I still think we should do a game show," Carolyn said, pouting.

"Why not do both?" said the Great Stoneybrook Ideas Machine.

Twin blank stares.

"I could read aloud for a while," Kristy went on. "You know, something short

and fun, like *Where the Wild Things Are*.
Then we could put on a *Jeopardy*-type
show—about kids' books! We provide the
answers, and the listeners call in to guess
the questions."

"Yes!" Carolyn shouted.

"But *Jeopardy* has categories," Marilyn
reminded them. "This is all one
category."

"Not necessarily," Kristy replied.
"We could have 'Books That Have Been
Made into Films', 'Romance Books',
'Mysteries'. . ."

"'Picture Books' and 'Chapter
Books'," Carolyn offered.

"And then, at the end," Marilyn said,
"we give the winner a grand prize, maybe
a holiday in Bermuda!"

"Er, it has to be something we can
afford," Kristy explained.

"A trip to Washington Mall?" Carolyn
said.

"I was thinking of a gift voucher for an
ice-cream sundae," Kristy suggested, "or
a cinema ticket."

"Oh, all right," Carolyn agreed.

"I want to ask the questions!" Marilyn
called out.

"You mean, give the answers," Carolyn
corrected her. "See, I'm the one who
knows how to play, so *I* should—"

"You can take turns," said Kristy the Peacemaker, rising from the playroom sofa. "Okay, we don't have much time. Let's get to work."

The three of them went into the kitchen. The twins found a pad and pencils in a drawer.

Over the next hour, Kristy and the girls chose five categories and thought up questions (I mean, *answers*) for each.

I saw them that Monday.

Ashley and I were bowled over. We were preparing our fifth show, and our topic was "What Are You Reading?"

Guess what?

We said yes. Kristy's dream had come true.

Maybe now she'd leave me alone.

13th CHAPTER

"Ready, Claudia? Ashley? Guests?" Mr Bullock asked from inside the glass booth.

"Ready," we replied.

"Ready, Mr Garber?"

Theodore "Ted" Garber, author of the spooky, creepy, gross, and super-popular series *Night Frights*, cleared his throat and said, "Ready!"

I was still in shock. The week before, Ashley had been dying to get a real, live author on the show. She'd heard that Mr Garber lived in Connecticut. On Friday she tried to invite him to the show, by calling his publishing company.

She did not expect that he'd call back on Saturday and say yes.

(I have to admit, I don't read *Night Frights*, but it felt very cool to be in the same room with a famous author.)

The engineer held up his arm. The red light went on. "Hello! It's a warm, gorgeous, fantastic Thursday, and welcome to 'For Kids Only'! This is Claudia Kishi, sitting with Ashley Wyeth, as always, and we have the coolest, most in*credible* show for you today!"

Not bad, huh? I was getting better and better at this stuff.

"Today's theme", Ashley continued, "is 'What Are You Reading'? Later we'll have a phone-in quiz show—a Junior *Jeopardy* based on kids' books. We'll also have Regina, Cathy and David, three seventh-graders who are collecting their own strange and spooky stories."

"And in the middle," I said, "for a full half an hour, we'll have our surprise guest, who will read from his new book, *Night Frights Number Thirteen: Don't Get Out of Bed!* Yes, fans, we have for you, here in the studio, live and in the flesh ... Mr Ted Garber!"

"*BOOO-AHHH-HAHH-HAAAHH!*"

I nearly jumped through the ceiling. Ashley let out a gasp.

Through the glass I saw the engineers sniggering and looking guilty. I suppose that was their idea of fun—scaring innocent people with unexpected spooky sound effects.

So weird. I just glared at them.

"Er, and now, take it away, Regina, Cathy and David!" Ashley said.

Mr Garber was smiling sympathetically at me. He looked as if he'd been scared, too (which I found very funny).

Well, the storytelling trio got off to a rocky start. (I think Mr Garber made them a little nervous.) But their final story was fantastic. It was called "Kokolimalayas, the Bone Man", a Native American tale about a boy who defeats a monster made of bones. Kokolimalayas sticks out his chest and defies the boy to shoot. But the boy knows the monster's secret: it's heart is in its fingertip. So he points his arrow and *zzzing!* 'Bye-'bye Bone Man!

"Bravo!" Mr Garber called out when they had finished.

They were thrilled by his response. They crowded around to shake his hand as I said, "And now, the guest you've all been waiting for: Misterrrr Ted Garrrrrberrr!"

(That was reverb. The engineers were in a wacky mood.)

"I wish I could talk like that," was the first thing Mr Garber said. "Maybe then my kids would listen to me."

He performed a funny routine, and

then started reading from his book. Off in the waiting room, I could see Kristy and the twins shuffling papers and fidgeting.

After the reading, we "opened the phones", and Mr Garber answered callers.

At precisely 5:45, Mr Garber finished off. I thanked him, gave Kristy a thumbs-up, and announced, "And now it's time for Junior *Jeopardy* with Kristy Thomas, and the tremendous twins, Carolyn and Marilyn Arnold!"

Kristy confidently grabbed the mike and held it right up to her lips. "THOCK-HOO CLOFFFO!"

The engineer's eyes popped out. As they fiddled with dials, I gently pulled the mike farther away from Kristy's mouth.

"Welcome to Junior *Jeopardy*, the game of skill, smarts and speed!" Kristy said with a huge grin. "Get your pencils out while I read today's topics: Books Made into Films, Mysteries, Picture Books, Authors, and Timeless Classics. Each caller will pick a topic and we'll give you an answer to a question. If you guess the question, you get a second and third chance. Any caller who gives us three correct questions wins a cool prize! Let's take the first call."

She punched the speakerphone button. "Heyyyy, you're on the air with Kristy! Tell us your name and pick your category!"

(I know. What a ham!)

"Um, Sarah," a small voice replied. "I'll take Picture Books, please."

Marilyn looked down a sheet of A4 paper and leaned into the mike. "The famous elephant who is married to Queen Celeste," she said.

"*Babar!*" Sarah squealed.

"Answers must be in the form of a question," Kristy said solemnly.

"Who is Babar?" suggested Sarah.

"*Rrrrrrright!*" Kristy barked. "You go again!"

"Um—um—what were the other categories?"

Kristy patiently repeated them.

"Okay," Sarah said. "Timeless Classics."

Carolyn's turn. "In this book, three children step through a wardrobe into a wintry land ruled by a witch."

"What is . . . *The Wizard of Oz*?"

"Nooooo! We're sorry. The question is, What is *The Lion, the Witch, and the Wardrobe*?"

"But I haven't read that!" Sarah said.

"You should," was Kristy's reply. "It's great."

She flicked on the next caller. "What's *your* name?"

"Poindexter," a nasal voice said.

"And your category?"

"I pick . . . Kristy Thomas's nose!"

Kristy scowled. "Alan Gray, is that you?"

We heard a burst of wild laughter, then a click.

Typical.

The next caller chose Books Made into Films. Marilyn gave the answer: "She is the famous nanny who takes care of the Banks children."

"Who is Mrs Doubtfire!" the caller cried out.

"Nope," Kristy said. "Let's give another caller a chance." She pressed line 3. "Name, please."

"Mary Poppins!" the caller said. "I mean, Sandy Grayson. That's me. And . . . er, who is Mary Poppins?"

"Yyyyes! Pick another topic!"

"Mysteries."

Carolyn said, "Her best friend's name is Bess and she lives in the town of River—"

"Who is Nancy Drew?" Sandy blurted out.

(I only just held myself back from answering that one.)

"Yyyyes!" Kristy shouted.

"Authors." Sandy picked.

"He wrote *Jeremy Thatcher, Dragon Hatcher* and *Jennifer Murdley's Toad*," Marilyn said.

Silence.

Marilyn repeated the answer.

"Who is . . . Dr Seuss?"

"Nnnnoo! Next caller!"

"Who is Bruce Coville?"

"Yyyyyyou've got it!" Kristy replied. "What's your name and your next category?"

Kristy was flying. Carolyn and Marilyn looked as if they were having the time of their lives.

The fifteen minutes went by fast. The only embarrassing moment was when a caller didn't recognize one of Mr Garber's books.

Mr Garber grabbed a tissue and pretended to cry. We tried not to crack up. He's pretty cool.

Eventually three contestants did win prizes. When we finally ended the show, Kristy hopped around the room, whooping and pumping her fists.

"Eeeee! Eeeee! Eeeee!" Carolyn and Marilyn sounded like screaming parakeets as they hugged each other and jumped up and down.

The show which came on after ours was using a different studio, so Ash and I could hang around with Bob for a while after our guests left. We had already planned our sixth and seventh shows (themes: "Music" and "Hobbies"), but not our eighth.

I think we had been avoiding it. Number eight was our last.

The problem was, we hadn't used some of the talented kids who'd auditioned, because they hadn't fitted into any of our themes.

"I can think of themes for all of them," Ash said with a sigh. "But we'd need a few more shows. I wish we could just keep going."

"Me, too," I replied. "Maybe we could call the last show 'Weird Talents' or something. Just let it be a mixed bag of acts."

"You want my opinion?" Bob asked.

"Sure," I said.

"Your phone-in section—the one you did on the spur of the moment? Kids have been calling us, asking if you'll do it again."

"Great!" Ashley said. "We can do half

weird acts, and half 'Ask Dr Claudia'."

"No way," I said.

Ashley gave me a puzzled look. "Why not?"

"You mean, 'Ask Dr Claudia and Dr Ashley'," I reminded her.

Her face lit up. "It's a deal."

14th CHAPTER

"'Bye, Dad!" I called as the car drove away from the station.

"Good luck!" he replied.

Ash and I waved and watched him leave. Then we stood in the car park for a moment. Neither of us moved. We just stared silently at the squat, brick building.

Today was the Saturday of our last show. I didn't feel like rushing things, and I could tell Ashley didn't, either.

Everything had happened so fast. It was hard to imagine only a month had passed since I'd first met Mr Bullock. All my memories were so fresh. Frantically writing my essay. Sitting in Mr Bullock's office for the first time, petrified. Seeing Ashley walk in. Feeling absolutely horrified.

'Well, I suppose this is it," Ashley said softly. "Shall we?"

"Wait," I said. "I have a secret to tell you."

She turned towards me. Her eyes were moist. I could tell she was feeling just as nostalgic as I was.

"I didn't think this would work. The show, I mean. You and me trying to get along."

Ashley smiled. "Neither did I. No one told me you'd been the first-place winner. When Mr Bullock brought me into the office, I almost walked back out."

"I almost resigned."

We both nodded and looked at the ground. "Well," I said finally, "I feel really stupid about that now. I was wrong."

"Yeah. Me, too."

We shared a smile. Then we put our arms around each other's shoulders and walked into the station.

The door was unlocked, but the reception room was empty and the light was out.

"Are we early?" I asked.

"I don't think so," Ashley replied.

"Hey, there they are!" Mr Bullock's voice boomed into the room. He was standing in the corridor with a handful of cassettes and CDs.

"Sorry about the lights," he said. "Max

isn't here today. He's only working week-days now. Come on in."

As we walked past Mr Bullock's office, I noticed three cardboard boxes stuffed with old vinyl records and cassettes. Mr Bullock dropped his handful in a box. "We're clearing out some old stuff. Selling it to a collector." He sighed. "Gosh, I hate to see some of this stuff go."

Ash and I gave each other a Look. We knew why he was doing all this—cutting back Max's hours, selling old stuff. He needed to raise money for WSTO.

Either that or he'd just given up. Maybe he was going to sell the rest of the station's collection, too.

I hoped not. Bob had been running a tape of his editorial all week. His article had appeared in the Wednesday edition of the *Stoneybrook News*. It was very well written. Maybe help would soon be on the way.

"Bob, do you think we really need that third reel-to-reel machine?" Mr Bullock called into the conference room.

Then again, maybe not.

Bob bustled into the corridor. "Hi there! Ready for your swan song?"

Huh? I didn't remember any animal acts.

"Your last show," he explained.

133

"That's what swan song means. The song of the dying swan is supposed to be beautiful. How do you feel?"

"Like a dying swan," I said.

"We're totally depressed," Ashley added.

Bob smiled. "Uh-oh! They've been bitten by the bug. Watch out, radio world."

Together we went into the studio. The engineers, as usual, grunted hello and just kept on working. I wondered if they'd even realized how important this show was to us.

Then I found out.

"Claud," Ashley said, "where did this come from?"

I looked around her and saw a gorgeous bouquet of flowers on our table. "Wow!"

Ash found a card tucked inside. She held it out and read it aloud. "To the most wonderful radio hosts we have ever worked with, the WSTO engineers."

"*Should auld acquaintance be forgot. . .*"

Suddenly the schmaltzy old New Year's song was blaring over the studio speakers. The engineers had risen to their feet and were singing along, holding up glasses full of a clear, bubbly liquid. With a big smile,

Mr Bullock walked towards us with two glasses and a bottle of ginger ale.

I turned to Ashley. She turned to me. It was waterworks time. Tears galore.

Mr Bullock gave us a hug. We drank our ginger ale.

At the end of the song, Mr Bullock announced, "Okay, crew, we have a job to do!"

It was hard to get back on track. But soon the guests began arriving, and we had to greet them, prepare a sequence, and do all the other million things we'd learned to do before a show.

Our first guest was (finally) Sarah Sutton, the back-to-front talker. After that, we had four kids called the Curious Quartet, who played the banjo, the tin whistle, the Jew's harp and the washboard. Then Rob Miller, an eighth-grader from Stoneybrook Day School, told the strangest story: every time he reached a syllable that sounded like a number, he added *one* to it. (*Won*der became *two*der, *tou*can became *three*can, and so on.) He began the story, "Twice upon a time, there was a twoderful garden full of blossoming threelips." Ashley's favourite part was when a character said, "Elevennis, anytwo?"

I liked the no-structure approach to this

show. It was fun. I didn't have to keep thinking of a way to tie everything together.

At five-thirty I announced, "And now, welcome to Ask Dr Claudia. . ."

"And Dr Ashley," Ashley added.

I could see that all the lines were already lit up. I pressed line 1. "You're on the air."

"Er, hi, Claudia?" a boy's voice said.

"Yes?"

"Um, do you have. . ."

I could hear giggling in the background. Visions of Alan Gray danced through my head.

"Go on," I said.

"Do you have. . ."

More giggling. I reached for the button.

"A boyfriend?"

My hand froze.

So did my voicebox. I could feel my face going red. The engineers were cracking up. Luckily, the boy hung up before I had a chance to answer.

I quickly pushed line 2. "Hello?" My voice was a high-pitched squeak.

"Hi! My friends and I are taking a vote, and it's tied. Which is better, *The Lion King* or *Aladdin?*"

"*Aladdin*," I replied.

"*The Lion King*," Ashley said.

"Argggggggh!"

I resisted laughing.

"My name is Denise," said the next caller. "I have this little brother. And he's so gross sometimes. Like yesterday, when I had three friends here. He just comes into my room and sits down and starts burping. And he doesn't leave!"

"Have you tried talking to him about it?" Ashley asked.

"Yes. He answers in burp talk. It is so disgusting."

"You could all stare at him", Ashley suggested, "in total silence."

"He'll just keep doing it."

"Fine. Let him. And just keep staring. Silently. He'll leave, and I bet he won't come back for another try."

Brilliant. Ashley was brilliant. I would have told the girl to throw him out the window.

The next caller sounded as if he were about six years old. "Um, your show is *really* cool."

"Thanks," we answered.

Then, in a teeny, meek voice, he said, "Can both of you come to my house and babysit for me some time?"

Was I glad Kristy wasn't there! She'd have started grilling him for his address and his parents' names.

137

Me? I was moved. I said yes and gave him the BSC phone number.

A few calls later, a woman's voice said, "Hello, Claudia and Ashley. My name is Rhonda Hewitt."

"Hello," Ash and I said. The name sounded familiar, but I wasn't sure why.

"I know only children are supposed to call," the woman continued, "but as a mother of one of your callers, I thought this would be okay. My son, George, spoke to you a couple of weeks ago. You remember, the boy who was so upset about his parents separating?"

Hewitt! Of course. I started to feel faint. This could be big trouble. If I remembered correctly, George had said some not-so-nice things about his mum.

"I—" I had to swallow. "I remember."

I looked at the clock. Five fifty-eight. Yikes! What a way to end the last show.

"Well," Mrs Hewitt continued, "this, as you know, has been a very difficult time for him and my daughter. But I wanted to tell you that your suggestion was wonderful. You made a huge difference in his life. I wanted to thank you person-ally, and on the air."

Huh?

The cloud around my head was lifting. My stomach stopped slam-dancing inside my ribcage. "Oh," I said. "Thanks! I mean, you're welcome."

"I've also been hearing and reading about the station's financial trouble, and I think that's a horrible shame. So I'd like to make a donation. I've found your fax number and sent you a note on it. The cheque will follow in the post."

"Thank you so much, Mrs Hewitt," I said. "And I wish you the best of luck."

"My pleasure, dear. I wish there were more people like you. 'Bye, now!"

"'Bye."

Twenty seconds left. I felt as if I were floating. "Well, that's it for now. I want to thank Mr Bullock, Bob and our crazy engineers for all their help—"

"And all you great listeners!" Ashley said.

"*Especially* you," I agreed. "I hope you've enjoyed 'For Kids Only'. It's been a lot of fun for me."

"Me, too," Ashley said. "And don't forget, keep listening to WSTO!"

"Goodnight!"

"Goodnight!"

I felt a tug when that red light went off. Ashley and I stood up and gave each other a high-five. The engineers broke into applause.

Then the studio door opened, and Mr

Bullock rushed in, carrying a sheet of paper. On his face was a strange expression. "Everybody come and look at this," he called out.

Ashley, Bob, one of the engineers and I peered over his shoulder. It was the fax of Mrs Hewitt's note.

When I saw the amount of money she had pledged, my jaw nearly hit the floor.

"Wow!" Bob said under his breath. "I can see she must be pretty wealthy."

"That'll help the station, won't it?" Ashley asked.

Mr Bullock nodded. "If this pledge is for real," he said, "it'll keep us afloat for six months."

"YEEEEEAAAAA!" I screamed. (I couldn't help it.)

"Yyyyyes!" Ashley shouted.

"Hallelujah!" the engineer bellowed.

Bob? He sank quietly into a chair. From the look on his face, you'd think someone had told him he could eat ice cream three times a day for the rest of his life.

15th CHAPTER

"Claudia, phone for you," Mr Bullock called out. "On my office line."

I had been high-fiving staff members, helping Ashley clear our stuff out of the studio, and chatting happily about Mrs Hewitt's pledge. I excused myself and walked down the corridor to the station manager's office.

"Who is it?" I asked.

Mr Bullock just shrugged and left the room.

I picked up the receiver and said, "Hello?"

"Hi, Claudia? It's me."

She didn't have to say her name. I hadn't heard the voice in a long time (*too* long) but I'd recognize it anywhere.

"Stacey?" I said. All these feelings— anger, surprise, happiness—were staging a big wrestling match inside me. I didn't know what to say.

"Your show was great," Stacey remarked.

"You listened to it?"

"I've been listening to every single one, Claud. I thought they were all good. Especially the one about friendship."

"Oh? I ... mentioned you on that one."

"Yes. I heard."

Gulp! I had said something wrong. That was why she hadn't called me until now. She'd been insulted. "I—I'm sorry, Stace."

"Sorry about what?"

"Well, I mean, if you thought that was, you know, too private or something?"

"No, no, I loved it, Claudia. Really. I was so moved, I cried."

"Really?"

"Well, *yes*. I mean, all those things you said about friendship—they were so true. You really made me think, Claud. About all my friends and what they mean to me, who the most important people are in my life, stuff like that."

"Stacey, are you trying to tell me something? You didn't break up with Robert, did you?"

Stacey laughed. "No! I just, well, I just

hope we can be friends again one day. You and me. That's all."

"Yes," I said quietly. "Me, too."

Ashley appeared in the doorway with a stack of papers. She smiled and whispered, "When you have a chance, we need to go through these. I'll be in the studio."

"Er, Stace, I'd better go," I said into the phone. "See you."

"Okay. 'Bye! And congratulations."

"Thanks."

I walked out of the office and into the studio. The flowers were giving off the most wonderful smell. Ashley was sitting at the table, shuffling through papers with Bob. Next to her on the desk was an enormous Nestlé's Crunch bar with the words *For Claudia—With Love and Thanks, Ashley* written on a Post-It note stuck to it.

Ashley looked over her shoulder. "For energy. We still have some work to do."

I laughed. "Thanks, Ash."

I picked up the Crunch bar and sat at the table. I started to rip it open, but instead I just put it back down.

I didn't need it then.

I was feeling fine without it.

Look for No 86

MARY ANNE AND
CAMP BSC

We had a lull in the phones. Mal finished writing in the notebook. Claudia took a jujube and put it between two crisps and gulped it down.

I met Mal's eye. "Okay," I said. "We've got a potential problem ahead."

Kristy lifted her head like a bull who's seen a red flag. "What're you talking about? Is one of the kids we babysit having trouble?"

"Nope," I said. "The problem is summer."

"Summer is *never* a problem," said Claudia.

Dawn grinned. "I agree. The beaches are warm, school's finished, what could better?"

"Business is going to be better," said Mal. "Think about it!" She explained about camp and the community centre and the three week lag between that and the end of school. "Unless we take on more babysitters," she concluded, "we may have more work than we can handle."

"Wow, you're right Mal." Kirsty looked thoughtful.

"Who else can we get to work with us?" Shannon asked.

The silence built up. Claudia muttered something, then shook her head.

"I could ask some friends at my school if they could help out, but. . ." Shannon's voice trailed off.

Then Kristy's face lit up. "Camp," she said.

We waited.

"Camp," said Kristy again. "Camp BSC. A babysitters camp! A day camp! Like the mini-camp you and Dawn once had, Mary Anne."

It was perfect. We knew immediately that it would take care of the problem. If all eight of the current members of the BSC, including Logan and Shannon were counsellors, the camp could probably handle about twenty kids. And all our clients would be very happy.

"Perfect," I said aloud.

"Super perfect," echoed Claudia.

The phone ran again. And again. We were kept very busy the rest of the meeting setting up babysitting jobs.

It looked like the summer rush had already begun. We'd thought of the idea of Camp BSC just in the nick of time.

Goosebumps

R.L. Stine

Reader beware, you're in for a scare!
These terrifying tales will send shivers up your spine:

Goosebumps

Reader beware – you choose the scare!

Give Yourself Goosebumps

A scary new series from R.L. Stine – where *you* decide what happens!

Choose from over 20 scary endings!

HIPPO GHOST

Summer Visitors

Emma thinks she's in for a really boring summer,
until she meets the Carstairs family on the beach.
But there's something very *strange* about her
new friends...

Carol Barton

Ghostly Music

Beth loves her piano lessons. So why have they
started to make her *ill*...?

Richard Brown

A Patchwork of Ghosts

Who is the evil-looking ghost tormenting Lizzie,
and why does he want to hurt her...?

Angela Bull

The Ghosts who Waited

Everything's changed since Rosy and her family
moved house. Why has everyone suddenly
turned against her...?

Dennis Hamley

The Railway Phantoms

Rachel has visions. She dreams of two children
in strange, disintegrating clothes. And it seems
as if they are trying to contact her...

Dennis Hamley

Babysitters Little Sister

*Meet Karen Brewer. She's seven years old and her big sister Kristy
runs the Babysitters Club. And Karen's always having adventures
of her own… Read all about her in her very own series.*